BLOOD LUST!

"They may be making a move," Slocum said.

"Like what?" Findlay kept his gaze on the hotel.

"Slipping around to get us or your deputies."

Findlay shook his head. "Vermin like Ramey don't have the courage," he replied.

Slocum disagreed. "Men will do a lot of things to save their lives."

Suddenly, the sound of revolver fire came from the other side of the building...

The back door of the building was kicked open...

A barrage of bullets came whizzing into the room.

OTHER BOOKS BY JAKE LOGAN

JAKE LOGAN

GOLD FEVER

B

BERKLEY BOOKS, NEW YORK

GOLD FEVER

A Berkley Book/published by arrangement with
the author

PRINTING HISTORY
Berkley edition/ February 1989

ISBN: 0-425-11398-1

A BERKLEY BOOK ® TM 757,375
Berkley Books are published by The Berkley Publishing Group,
200 Madison Avenue, New York, N.Y. 10016.
The name "BERKLEY" and the "B" logo
are trademarks belonging to Berkley Publishing Corporation.

PRINTED IN THE UNITED STATES OF AMERICA.

10 9 8 7 6 5 4 3 2 1

1

Sally Ryan had been in Cheyenne—a lusty Wyoming cow town—for three weeks. Now, on a cool spring afternoon on the second day of April, Sally removed her clothes in her room at the Cattleman's Hotel. Once, twice, she ran her delicate hands over the smooth contours of her shapely hips.

Smiling, Sally crossed the room and posed in front of a full-length wall mirror. She smiled at her attractive, curvaceous nude image in the glass. She wasn't a spring pullet anymore, she decided, but her packaging was good for a few more years. Exercise, good food, moderate habits, and milk baths would keep the wrinkles and worry lines at a distance.

"Sally Ryan, you're a prize," she told her reflection.

Her statement was not conceit, but an assessment by an attractive young woman of her physical attributes. Twenty-five years old, Sally was noted for her long wheat-colored hair. The yellow strands cascaded over her bare shoulders, framing a pretty face with fine, pleasing features. Her beauty was enhanced by theatrical makeup that created a beguiling, girlish look of innocence.

Now the gaze from Sally Ryan's smoke-gray eyes drifted down to her breasts. White and round, nipples pink and tumescent, she was grateful for these twin endowments. She accepted her breasts as part of Mother Nature's goodness; those two fleshy melons enabled her to earn good money as an entertainer.

She raised her hand and gently strummed her sensitive nipples. The light pressure of her fingers created a glowing warmth. Sighing, she cupped her breasts, raised them high. Then she released the flesh and watched the bobbing effect. The round firmness of her flesh held a thrusting upward tilt.

She turned and stared at the nude profile of her body in the mirror. Her stomach and abdomen were tanned expanses of soft skin that fell away to a triangular patch of blond hair. She fluffed the hair with a gentle caress. Lightly, she stroked the tender flesh of her clitoris with quickening breath. So nice, so sensitive.

Without warning, a harsh knock sounded on the door of her hotel room.

"Just a second," she called.

Sally grabbed a black silk gown and belted the garment around her waist. She hurried over and opened the door.

Sally Ryan's face brightened. "John Slocum!" Her voice was warm, passionate. "You're back! You don't know how I've missed you! I'm hot and ready for an afternoon of loving."

John Slocum leaned against the outside frame of the door. He was a lean man, six feet one inch tall, with hair as dark as the underside of a raven's wing. Slocum was dressed in buckskin trousers and a fringed over-shirt. Two Colt Navy pistols rested in the holsters on his hips.

Slocum smiled and tipped the brim of his black, flat-crowned sombrero. "Ma'am, I'm earning money for higher education by selling subscriptions to *The Proper Woman's Monthly Guide*. College will change my life. I'm schooling to learn if the Cheyenne and the Arapahoe are kin to the lost tribes of Israel."

Sally Ryan giggled. "Honey, I'm bare as a babe under this robe. If you want an education, come through the door. I've got something that'll change your life. Get in here! I'm horny!"

"I'd love to come into your room, ma'am." John Slocum leaned against the doorframe. "I like that part about you being naked. I'll bet you're a lady, all the way from toe to tit. Get what I mean?"

"Quit teasing or you're getting nothing," said Sally Ryan in a pouting tone.

"My boss said never to give in to the temptations of a naked woman."

"Your boss is crazy, John," Sally's tone was low and provocative.

Slocum went on, "My boss says improper women will sooner or later want to get into unspeakable acts."

"All right, John. Come inside and I'll perform a vast repertoire of unspeakable acts on you."

Slocum cleared his throat. His eyes narrowed, and he looked around with mock suspicion. "Ma'am, you claiming to have an acquaintance with carnal knowledge?"

Sally grinned. "We're old friends. Carnal and I have buddied together many a time. Come on, John. I've been thinking about doing it."

"Well, I—" Slocum began.

"Don't pull that aw-shucks-folks routine on me," Sally said. She grabbed Slocum's arm and pulled him into the room.

Slocum's gaze swept over Sally Ryan's attractive figure. "You're almost as pretty as Matilda," he said.

Jealousy shimmered in Sally Ryan's smoke-gray eyes. "Who's Matilda?" she demanded.

"A female sheep up in Spotted Knee, Wyoming."

Sally giggled. "I'm sure she is the fairest companion in Spotted Knee."

"The boys say she's right nice."

"Quit teasing," Sally Ryan complained. "I've got a couple of hours, then I have to get ready for my show."

John Slocum unbuckled his gunbelt and hung the holstered pistols over a bedpost. Sally Ryan pressed her body close, opened her lips, and nibbled his ear.

"You're a lusty wench," Slocum said.

"And you're a lucky man," Sally replied, unbuttoning his shirt. She pulled off the garment, planting wet kisses on Slocum's chest.

Sally Ryan was anxious to get into bed. John Slocum was one of the most expert lovers Sally Ryan had ever known. He was different from the usual men—a lover who knew instinctively what a woman wanted.

Sally Ryan and five chorus girls were billed as a road company of all-star entertainers. Their appearances were booked through a Chicago agent, who provided entertainment to saloons, theaters, dancing halls, agricultural fairs, and exhibitions. The troupe had roamed across west Texas, Colorado, Missouri, Nebraska, Montana, Illinois, northern Michigan, and were now appearing in the boomtowns of the frontier West.

They traveled by train or stagecoach, stayed in the

best hotels and boardinghouses, or slept in tents if housing was scarce in a boomtown. Sally and her girls had been in Cheyenne for almost a month, appearing at a local music hall. The theater was crammed each night with cowboys, mostly young men still in their teens, who were seeing a stage show for the first time.

Soon the troupe would leave Cheyenne for a series of appearances in South Dakota. Sally Ryan had lost one girl during the tour of Wyoming. A pretty redheaded dancer had fallen in love with a cowpoke, left the show, and rode off to ranch in western Nebraska.

Now, Sally Ryan pulled back the satin coverlet on the bed. She dropped her black robe and slipped between the sheets.

John Slocum sat down on the edge of the bed. He pulled off his boots as Sally Ryan snuggled against him.

Slocum stood up, unbuckled his belt, and let his jeans drop to the floor.

Sally Ryan inhaled sharply. "God, you're ready," she husked. "That's bigger than I've ever seen it."

"I've been thinking about you," Slocum said. Thoughts about Sally Ryan had occupied Slocum's mind during a stagecoach run back from Nebraska. He had sat on the seat beside the driver, shotgun cradled in his arm, his thoughts focused on the bedroom antics with Sally on arrival in Cheyenne.

"Glory, mister. You should have been a lancer in the Army."

Slocum grinned. "Now, how many years of magazine subscriptions will you buy?"

The young woman's hand fastened on his hardness. "Get in bed," she smiled, "and I'll take a lifetime subscription."

Slocum lay down beside Sally Ryan. Her nimble

fingers worked against him. He glanced down and her globular breasts looked like ivory mounds tipped with a glowing pinkness.

Slocum kissed one breast, then the other. His tongue moved easily up and down the warm flesh. Sally made a purring sound deep down in her throat. She thrust her breasts up for more attention. Slocum took one of her pink nipples between his lips and let his tongue slither over the jutting hardness.

Sally Ryan's fingers were working on his manhood. She clasped his rigid flesh between her fingers, pulling up and down with a tightening intensity. Then she twisted onto her side and brought him against the moist wetness at the apex of her slender legs.

The noise deep inside Sally's throat became louder, a deep humming sound of pleasure. She responded easily as Slocum pressed her back against the sheets. Hungrily, she looked up into his eyes as the man from Calhoun County, Georgia, moved above her.

Then Sally's legs opened wide and Slocum caught a glimpse of moist pink flesh. He maneuvered his body and pressed forward with his rigid flesh. Sally Ryan closed her eyes as Slocum's stiffness penetrated her body.

"All of it!" Sally pleaded. "Every bit! All the way, baby!"

Slocum moved forward a few inches as the woman wiggled to accept him. He felt the warmth of Sally's flesh surround him with a moistness that excited him even more. Then he rocked forward on his knees and penetrated more deeply into her body.

Sally Ryan let out a tiny cry.

"Am I hurting you?" Slocum asked. He was afraid of injuring the young entertainer.

"God, no! Give me more," she moaned. "Fill me up, John! All the way!"

"You can't take any more," he said.

"I got to have it, baby!" A frantic urgency came into Sally's voice. "Having you inside me is so good! So good!"

Carefully, John Slocum moved forward another inch. Every thrust made Sally Ryan gasp with pleasure. She begged for more of his rigid flesh, pleaded with a moaning little cry that echoed the hunger of her body. Then she twisted her bottom, and that opened her inner being to John Slocum. He began a smooth, rhythmic thrusting motion that heightened Sally's desire.

Slocum rocked to and fro until Sally gasped, thrust upward, and locked her legs around his waist. Then she encircled his neck with her arms as he moved quicker, more powerfully, till the force of their lovemaking caused Slocum to groan and release his throbbing ardor.

The young woman groaned too with pleasure and tightened her arms and legs around him. Then they both lay still. They were spent, exhausted by their mutual lust.

Sally Ryan looked up into Slocum's face with a pleasant smile. "Thank you kindly, dear sir!"

"My pleasure!" Slocum smiled.

"And it has been that," Sally agreed. She brushed her lips against his chin. "Dear John, you're great in bed. I've never had a man as good as you."

"Yeah," Slocum agreed with mock conceit. "All the ladies tell me that."

"Braggart!" Sally Ryan's long fingernails scraped lightly over the skin of his arm.

Slocum kissed the end of her nose. "Always remember, Sally, that it takes two to make it good."

"Thank you, sir." She wiggled against him.

John Slocum gave her another kiss, then rose from the bed and washed himself in a basin sitting on the dresser. Then he pulled on his clothes and put on his gunbelt, tying down the holsters.

Sally Ryan watched Slocum with a languid contentment. "Are you happy?" she asked.

Slocum nodded. "As much as any man, I suppose. I have a pretty girl, two sets of clothes, a pair of boots that don't leak. I'm working regularly, and the food is pretty good around here."

"What about the future?"

"Does this have anything to do with getting married?"

Sally laughed. "No, I'm not trying to weasel a proposal. I want to make you a deal."

"I'm always willing to listen."

"You've been in Cheyenne for how long?"

"Several weeks," he said.

"What are your plans?"

"I don't look too far into the future."

"Would you like to join my show?"

Slocum pulled a small chair up to the bed. He sat down and looked at the girl. He took a moment to reply. "I can't sing, dance, or act."

Sally Ryan sat up in bed, her gray eyes gazing into Slocum's face. "What I want is a stud, Slocum. He'd have to be a special man. I didn't think he existed until I met you."

"I'm not a gigolo."

"Look, running an all-girl show isn't easy. Especially when you make these western cow towns. Every man who buys a ticket wants to take one of my girls to bed, marry them, or whatever."

"Sally, that's human nature. Men hanker for good women. Your girls are pretty and entertaining. They're a prize out here. I know men who would kill for one of your girls."

"My girls are crazy for men," Sally responded. "They're normal young women who need their ashes hauled on a regular basis."

"I see," John said. "I'm to be the official chimney sweep?"

"I prefer the official Sally Ryan stud service. When me or the girls get the yen for bedroom action, we have John Slocum to care for our needs."

The job offer was interesting, a tantalizing opportunity that appealed to John Slocum. Sally Ryan and her young women were attractive young women, noted for their beauty throughout the frontier. Besides good looks, members of the troupe were picked for their pleasing personalities and intelligence.

Slocum bolted upright on the bed. He looked at Sally Ryan with a wide-eyed gaze. "You want me to be a kept man for six women? I may be kind of slow, Sally, but I ain't crazy."

"I've got everything figured out," she said. "We've been making love in the afternoon and again at night. That's twice a day. This means you could handle me and the other five girls every three days. None of the girls will get antsy and run off with some galoot. They'll be taken care of wherever we appear."

Slocum was thoughtful for a moment. "The girls would get jealous," he said at last.

Sally Ryan shook her head negatively. "We're not talking about love. This is a physical thing."

"There would still be problems."

"We'll work them out when the time arrives."

"I'll have to think about it."

Sally leaned over and pressed her lips against Slocum's cheek. "Other men would jump at the chance."

Slocum grinned. "A couple of weeks and they'd be too tired to jump."

"Besides, I don't want to break up this friendship," Sally added, gently running her hand over the tight muscles of Slocum's chest. "We've got a good thing going. I need you around me. The girls need someone to talk to besides me. You could be father, lover, and adviser. You'll never get another offer like this one."

Slocum laid his head back on the pillow. He pulled Sally close to him, felt the softness of her breasts against his body. "I appreciate it," he said. "But something like that never works. I'd be a kept man, dependent on a paycheck from you."

"Not true." Sally moved her hips against him. "All you're doing is riding shotgun on the stagecoach from here to Julesburg. That's a waste of talent."

"I'll think about it."

Sally's laugh was loud and filled with pleasure. "Don't think about it, Slocum. Think about all of those girls lined up in a row, bottoms up, ready and waiting for you. Wall-to-wall poontang! The sight would make a man drool with delight. Every man west of the Mississippi will envy you. You'll be known as the man with a golden pecker."

He drew her face down to him, kissed her.

"Sloppy seconds?" she husked.

Slocum was considering the possibility when he heard the sound of hooves pounding outside on the street. The man from Georgia walked over to the window of the hotel room. He pulled back the velvet curtain and looked down into the street.

Six horsemen were pulling up at the hitching post in front of the local bank. They were men with rugged features, and they swung down from their saddles like trail-weary hardcases. They laid the reins of their horses across the hitching rail, untied. One man stood with his back turned away from Slocum's view. He held a rifle cradled in his arms. The five other men walked into the bank building.

"What's happening?" Sally asked.

"Trouble," Slocum said. "Five men just walked into the bank."

"Maybe they're depositors," Sally said.

Slocum's voice was quick, sharp. "These gents are planning a fast withdrawal."

"A bank robbery?" Sally came alert, sitting up in the bed.

At that moment, the outside man turned around and Slocum caught a view of his face.

Brazos Tyler!

Alarm bells went off in Slocum's mind.

He let the curtain fall back into place.

Then, wheeling around on his boot heel, Slocum started for the door.

"Don't try and stop them!" Sally cried. She reached out and grabbed Slocum's wrist.

He paused. "Let me go," he snapped. "I have to kill a man."

2

John Slocum jerked open the door of Sally Ryan's hotel room. He rushed out into the corridor, then pounded down the stairs leading to the lobby. Two salesmen from Omaha were sitting on a sofa near the window. They looked around with alarmed expressions as Slocum came charging down into the lobby.

One of the drummers started to speak. His lips moved, but only a tiny, squeaking sound came from his mouth.

John Slocum ignored the man and moved through the lobby to a side door that led out into an alley. The spring air was cold enough to turn Slocum's breath into mist. He slowed his pace, walked to the end of the alley, and glanced across the street toward the bank.

Across the way, waiting with the horses, was Brazos Tyler. Tyler was a stocky man of medium height. He was wearing a sheep-lined coat with the collar pulled up over his thick neck. His face was hard-featured, almost primitive in appearance. A broad, red slash from an old knife fight scarred his left cheek.

The outlaw paced to and fro on the wooden sidewalk in front of the bank. His gaze swept up and down the street looking for any sign of an outcry. He held his repeating rifle in an easy way, keeping the weapon pointed down, the barrel close to his legs. A casual passerby might not notice that Brazos Tyler was armed and ready to kill.

Slocum slumped his shoulders and relaxed his posture. He came out of the alley and walked across the street with a shuffling motion. Brazos Tyler was a renegade who wouldn't want to alarm the town. Slocum knew that the getaway was the most dangerous part of a bank robbery. Gunfire could alert the citizens in town, and bullets might start flying like swarming bees.

Slocum shambled across the street with an easy-gaited looseness. He tried to look like a man headed home to sleep off a drunken spree. Slocum kept his head down on his chest, snubbing the toe of his boot to look like a drunk.

Brazos Tyler wanted to avoid gunplay during the robbery. Warily, the outlaw watched as the dumb saddlebum stumbled across the street. The guy had really tied one on, Tyler thought.

Then Slocum shambled up on the sidewalk about fifteen paces from where Tyler stood.

"Get away from here!" snapped Tyler in a guttural tone. "Go sleep it off, rummy!"

Slocum raised his head and stared at the outlaw.

"Remember me, Tyler?" His voice was hard, firm.

The outlaw looked at Slocum with an expression of half horror, half surprise. His mouth dropped open. For an instant, Tyler tried to remember where his trail had crossed with Slocum. Then his face mirrored the knowledge that the man from Georgia was an enemy connected to the past.

Tyler's scarred face twisted into a wolfish grin. "Here's to you, Slocum!" the outlaw snarled. He started to bring up the rifle for a fast hip-level shot.

"Drop it, Tyler!" Slocum yelled, going into a crouch as he drew his Navy Colt revolver. The gun belched as it cleared leather in the fast motion of rolling lightning. The acrid smell of powder assailed Slocum's nostrils.

The bullet struck Brazos Tyler in the chest. The power of the lead slug knocked the outlaw sideways. His body shook with a spastic motion, like a dog shaking off water. His back hit the top of the hitching post.

His eyes were flint hard with hatred. Although the outlaw's scarred face was twisted with pain and anger, he did not go down. With black fury etched on his face, Brazos Tyler tried to raise the rifle to shoot Slocum.

Slocum fanned the hammer of his gun with his left palm.

The slug smashed into Brazos Tyler's scarred face.

The outlaw's twitching body was held up by the hitching post. His finger tightened in a death grip on the trigger of the rifle. The weapon's barrel was pointed down toward the wooden sidewalk. The rifle cracked, and the bullet smashed into the plank walkway.

The three shots had been a booming, staccato roar that seemed like a single, prolonged firing.

Bedlam broke loose in Cheyenne.

The shots spooked the horses belonging to the outlaw gang. A big roan stallion reared up, his front hooves pawing the air. A brown and gray paint spun around and slammed into the hitching post. Shocked faces began to appear in the windows of the hotel across the street.

Two men peered out of the doorway of a barbershop next to the bank.

A gunshot boomed inside the bank.

A shrill scream sounded as the front window of the bank building shattered.

Slocum stepped across the dead body of Brazos Tyler. He raced along the sidewalk toward the safety of the barbershop and had just barely stepped into the doorway of the small clapboard building as the five bandits tore out of the bank.

A wiry man with a scarred face stood on the sidewalk holding a long-barreled revolver. "Get the horses," he yelled.

"Who shot Brazos?" croaked an old man carrying a double-barreled Greener shotgun.

"Shut up!" The tall man was angry. "Get those animals before they take off."

A moon-faced youngster in a leather coat came out of the bank lugging two money bags. He grabbed the reins of the nearest horse and started to swing up into the saddle. The animal reared up, front hooves clawing the air. Then the kid jerked on the reins and the animal came down on all four hooves. The horse started to leap up again, but the young man took a tight grip on the bridle. The kid started to mount the horse. He put one foot into the stirrup, but the animal shied and spun around.

That was the instant when he saw Slocum standing in the doorway of the barbershop. The man from Georgia had his revolver pointed in the kid's direction. All Slocum had to do was squeeze the trigger and the young man was headed for Boot Hill. Then Slocum shrugged and lowered the barrel of his gun. The moon-faced kid smiled, leaped up into the saddle, and rode off at a fast gallop.

The other robbers milled around in the street trying to grab a horse.

A bespectacled bank clerk's face appeared in the window frame of the bank building. He raised an old flintlock pistol at the bandits milling around in the street. The clerk squeezed off a round. His lead missed the men and horses and slammed into the front window of the hotel across the way. The big glass pane of the hotel window broke into tiny slivers and pieces.

The old man in the gang cursed, spun around, and let loose with both barrels of the Greener shotgun. The barrage of buckshot almost tore the head off the bank clerk's body. The old man cackled a roar of laughter. Nervelessly, the old man stood in front of the bank and reloaded his weapon. Only then did the bandit amble over and crawl on a big-bellied red mare.

Meanwhile, Slocum slipped into the barbershop. The barber and his frightened customer cowered when he came into the room. The customer was a long-necked man with shaving lather on the right side of his face.

"D-don't shoot," stuttered the barber.

"I'm not with the gang," Slocum snapped. He kept his revolver at the ready as he glanced out the doorway.

Once the gang was mounted, they raced down the street at a thundering pace. Their departure from Cheyenne had barely started when a white-haired man stepped out into the street. He wore a silver badge on his vest. He raised a shotgun to his shoulder and took aim. The bandits let loose a stinging hornet's nest of lead. The sheriff was dead before his body fell onto the ground.

The gang rode toward the north as fast as their big

horses could run. They reined up a couple of miles outside of Cheyenne. The horses were winded; they gasped
for breath through their wide flared nostrils. When their
animals were rested, the gang split up into two groups.
They set out at an easy gallop toward their hideout.

The town of Cheyenne was in turmoil.

The president of the bank was dead. He had pulled a
hideout gun from a desk drawer with his shaking hands.
His bullet had slammed into the window behind one of
the robbers. The banker was shot by the angry gang.
The bank clerk who had taken a potshot at the gang was
dead from the old man's shotgun blast. So was the sheriff, who had walked out into the middle of the street. He
had been brave enough to try and prevent the gang's
getaway, and foolish enough to stand unprotected in the
street.

Meanwhile, John Slocum was sitting alone at the
back table in the Cattleman's Saloon sipping a beer. The
man from Georgia had gone back to Sally Ryan's room
after the shoot-out with Brazos Tyler. The young
woman entertainer was frightened and shocked. Slocum
helped Sally prepare for her performance at the
Cheyenne Opera House that evening. He left her at the
stage door and went into the saloon for a beer.

Slocum had been working as a shotgun guard on a
stagecoach running from Cheyenne to western Nebraska's cow towns. Although the railroads had laid
tracks into the frontier, many towns were served solely
by stagecoaches. Slocum's job as a shotgun guard was a
temporary arrangement until something interesting came
along.

Now, sipping his beer, the man from Georgia was
deep in thought. His eyes were focused distantly, his

mind automatically shutting out the conversation from drinkers at the bar. A half-dozen men were bellied up to the walnut bar, talking about the bank robbery and drinking whiskey. Slocum had not been connected to the shoot-out in front of the bank. He had gone to Sally Ryan's room in the hotel when the outcry started.

Slocum was about ready to order another beer when a rangy man in a dark suit walked into the saloon. The stranger waited until the barman served refills to two cattlemen. Then the stranger leaned his sun-darkened face over the bar and whispered in the bartender's ear. The bartender motioned his head toward the table where Slocum sat.

The stranger walked toward Slocum with a confident step. His boots were black, polished to a sheen, and the heels made a harsh sound on the barroom floor. Slocum judged the man to be in his late thirties, maybe early forties. He had a sharp nose that was slightly twisted toward the tip, as if it had been broken and set awkwardly after a fight. The stranger's forehead was creased with deep lines. His heavy brows were thick above two sharp, alert brown eyes.

He wore a black leather gunbelt and holster. His Colt revolver, worn low and tied down on his right hip, had carved white bone handles. Altogether, the stranger made an impressive figure, and Slocum wondered what he wanted.

Slocum's thumb played across the top of his beer glass as the man came up.

"Mr. Slocum?"

The man from Georgia nodded. "John Slocum."

"J. J. Findlay," the man said. "I'm the U.S. marshal for this neck of the woods. Mind if I sit down for a minute? I got a few questions to ask you about the shoot-out this afternoon."

"Sure, have a seat," Slocum replied. "I doubt I can help you."

"Colman the barber said you were around the bank this afternoon," said Findlay.

"I didn't have anything to do with the robbery."

Findlay raised his hand, palm toward Slocum. "Don't get touchy, mister. I know who robbed the bank. Leastways, I will after I finish talking with you. Right now, we got a dead body over at Newman's Funeral Home. All laid out on a slab because someone put out his lights during the bank robbery. He's an ugly-looking cuss with a face that would stop a clock. He's got a bullet in his chest and part of his head has been shot off. The barber said you were the gentleman who did the shooting."

"What if I did?"

"Well, you'd probably get a good citizen's award," said the marshal. "Killing a man helping rob a bank isn't a crime. I just figured that the man who shot him might know his name. It ain't nothing I'm going to lose sleep over. But Uncle Sam likes to keep track of which hardcase has gone to the great beyond."

Slocum was wary. "Assuming I'm the man who shot him."

"The barber says so."

"Eyewitnesses get things confused."

"Another beer?" Findlay motioned to the bartender for service. "You see, Slocum, I think this was the Ramey gang. Bart Ramey's been riding roughshod over folks for about three years. Most gangs last for a couple months, maybe a year. The Dalton boys were out for about fourteen months before the citizens of Coffeyville, Kansas, put them to rest. Ramey's a sharp hombre. It'll help me if I know he's bringing in hardcases from outside Wyoming. I figure the dead man was a newcomer with the gang."

"That might be right," Slocum agreed.

Findlay looked up as the bartender came over wiping his hands on the hem of his white apron.

"A couple of beers," Findlay told the barkeep. He turned to Slocum. "I telegraphed a couple of places after the barber told his story. I should know later tonight if there are any wanted posters out on you."

"I'm not wanted," Slocum said.

"Good. Of course, that's what everyone says. I hate to hassle a man, but I have to do it. What is the dead man's name?"

"Tyler. He's called Brazos. I don't know his real first name."

"You ever see him before today?"

"Texas."

"What year?"

"About three years ago."

"Was he riding the owlhoot trail back then?"

Slocum started to answer, then waited until the bartender sat their beers on the table and took payment from J. J. Findlay.

Slocum picked up his beer, held it up toward the U.S. marshal. "To your health, sir," Slocum said.

"And yours," grinned Findlay. He blew a quarter inch of foam off his drink onto the floor. "Now, about this jasper with his lights put out."

"He was running with a bunch of comancheros when I met him."

"Renegades?"

"Worse than anything in this part of the country,"

said Slocum. "This bunch were cold-blooded murderers. They killed for the fun of seeing someone suffer. A pardner and I got jumped by Tyler and his bunch."

"You don't look the type to get ambushed," said Findlay.

"I was careless that night. They slipped into camp when we were sleeping. We were miles from nowhere out on the prairie, so we didn't figure we needed to stand guard. I made a mistake that night. They were all around the camp before I woke up. Mexicans, half-breeds, Tyler, and a couple of Comanches. A bad bunch."

Findlay took a sip of his beer. "I've met a few like that. Vermin on two legs. Animals who look like men."

"Animals just kill to eat. The comancheros killed my partner. Staked him out on the ground, built a fire between his legs, and laughed as he screamed."

"That's inhuman."

"My partner died slow and hard," said Slocum. "The man who thought of doing that to my friend was Brazos Tyler."

Findlay asked, "How did you escape?"

"We were crossing the plains with a cartload of whiskey. We'd been up in Taos and planned on selling whiskey for a profit down in Texas. They got into the whiskey by the time my partner died."

J. J. Findlay's eyebrows lowered. "You escaped?"

"I didn't sell out to them," Slocum said testily. "They took my clothes, staked me out, and poured some molasses over me. Then, laughing all the while, they rode off."

"You escaped?"

"They were drunk when they tied me to the stakes."

"You were lucky."

"I got loose, walked to a ranch about forty miles away, got some clothes, and rested up. The rancher could have won an award for the tightest man in the West. I had to dig fence holes for two months to pay for an old gun and a broken-down horse."

"You ever see Tyler since then?"

"No. He would've been dead before Cheyenne if our trails had crossed."

Findlay raised his eyebrows. "You don't take kindly to murderers?"

"That's right. I don't."

J. J. Findlay finished his beer. "Well, Brazos Tyler is a dead man now. I'll check around. There may be a reward out for him. You might make some money."

"Seeing him die was payment enough," Slocum said.

Findlay agreed. "You get a good look at the gang when they charged out of the bank?"

"There were five of them besides Tyler."

"An old man among them, maybe?" asked Findlay.

"A real rattlesnake. He fired a double-barreled Greener into the bank coming out."

"Which killed a man," said Findlay. "That had to be old Rafe Miller."

"I've never seen him before," Slocum said. "How come you're sitting here talking with me? You should be heading up a posse and going after the gang."

Findlay smiled. "No need for that. I got a tip a couple of days ago. It didn't seem like much at the time, more like the rantings of a drunken whore who'd been mistreated. Now it all fits in. The gang has been in town for a couple days casing the bank. One of the bandits got drunk and mouthy. He told the chippie where he was going to hide out."

"That should make your job an easy one."

"Maybe," grunted Findlay. "Where are you staying?"

"Mrs. O'Brien's boardinghouse. Across the tracks by the rail yard."

"I know the place," said Findlay. "Be ready to leave about seven tomorrow morning."

Slocum frowned. "I'm not riding with any posse."

"Neither am I," Findlay explained. "Citizens don't make good lawmen."

"You're right," Slocum agreed.

"They get too eager when the odds are fifty to one."

"And they can't be counted on when the showdown comes," added Slocum. "Maybe I don't want to ride with a big posse, Findlay. But I'm not about to start a manhunt for the gang by the two of us."

Findlay nodded. "I've got a couple of good deputies, Slocum. They'll be going along. The four of us should be able to clean out that gang of thieves before the week is out."

3

John Slocum was eating breakfast at the boardinghouse when J. J. Findlay showed up the next morning at seven o'clock. Findlay graciously refused Mrs. O'Brien's offer of breakfast. The lawman accepted a cup of coffee from the landlady, sat, and chatted until Slocum finished eating.

The two men rode into downtown Cheyenne, where Slocum left a note for Sally Ryan. Then they stopped at the livery stable and picked up a pack mule loaded with supplies for their trip. Their next stop was at the U.S. marshal's office. Two of Findlay's deputies were waiting on a bench in front of the office. They were both large men with muscular arms, and they had the look of men who would not hesitate to kill if the situation called for gunplay.

The group left Cheyenne and followed the trail left by the robbers. Findlay reported the bandits would be holed up in an isolated area about a day's ride from Cheyenne. It was an area called Paradise Valley. That

part of Wyoming was the site of an out-of-the-way
ghost town. Bandits, lawbreakers, and general ne'er-
do-wells hung around Paradise Valley.

"Some pioneers came out here and decided to set up
a town in there," Findlay explained. "It turned out to be
the worst idea in history. The water is plentiful, the
grass fairly good, but the location is too isolated. They
hung on for a few years, then drifted away. They left a
few good houses, a corral and livery stable, and a few
other buildings. Being so far away from everything, it
was natural that the hardcases would use the place for a
hideout."

They rode until noon, stopping by a small stream and
eating beef jerky while the horses rested. Slocum noticed that Findlay and the other two men tended to their
horse first. That was a good sign of a man's character,
Slocum figured, because they knew the value of horseflesh in the wilderness.

They rode steadily that afternoon and, a half hour
before sunset, stopped by a small pond to camp for the
night. Findlay started a campfire while Slocum went off
in search of live game. The fire was blazing when he
came back into camp with two prairie chickens. Findlay
opened two cans of beans, added some molasses, and
warmed the mixture over the fire.

They ate as the sun vanished behind the western horizon. The two deputies finished their meal, took their
bedrolls, and went off to sleep away from the camp.
They didn't intend being surprised by unexpected visitors during the night. Slocum and Findlay stayed by the
campfire and talked.

Slocum learned that Findlay was from Pennsylvania,
the son of a farmer who raised cattle. Findlay had
served as an artilleryman in the Union army. He had

been in some of the hardest battles of the Civil War.

"Did you have trouble settling down after the war?" Slocum asked.

"I still have a problem," admitted the marshal. "Anyone with the sense of a prairie dog would be comfortable by the time they're my age. I'll be forty years old next month. Most men my age have a wife and family. But you're right. The war changed things for me. I can't handle a routine like other people. I'm an honest man. That meant I became a U.S. marshal instead of an outlaw. Where were you raised?"

Slocum mentioned his boyhood on the family farm in Georgia, his enlistment in the Confederate army, and the loss of a brother during the battle of Gettysburg. "I guess it was a natural thing for me to drift west," he said. "Out here, a man can make his own luck."

"You ought to be a lawman," Findlay said. "I had a couple of telegrams come in last night. One was from a sheriff in Colorado and the other was sent by the U.S. marshal in Kansas City. They say you're a fairly respectable man and a good hand with a gun."

Slocum laughed. "Findlay, I've got friends who would die from shock if they saw a tin badge on the front of my shirt."

"That sheriff in Colorado also mentioned you'd been in some wild escapades in the past."

"He's just listening to rumors," Slocum laughed.

"We're always looking for good men," the marshal went on. "The West is filling up fast with trashy people. Judges in the eastern states are giving prisoners a choice: leave town, head west, or go to prison. That brings a lot of hardcases out here. A person would have to be crazy to pick prison on a deal like that."

"Maybe most of those prisoners just need a new

chance. One thing I like about the West is the way people can start a new life," Slocum said. "A man isn't
judged on his family name, whether he has money, or
whether his daddy is rich. None of that matters if you
pull your own weight."

"True," agreed Findlay.

"When the West gets settled we're going to lose
that."

"I'd hate to imagine the whole country being sur-
veyed, plotted, and fenced in like Pennsylvania." Findlay picked up his tin dish. "I'm going to turn in. We got
a hard day tomorrow."

The next morning, Slocum and the three lawmen rode
up on a mountain overlooking Paradise Valley. J. J.
Findlay held up his hand and the men stopped in a copse
of trees on a rimrock overlooking the valley. The two
deputies walked back to the pack mule and came back
carrying Winchester carbines. Slocum pulled his Winchester from his scabbard.

Findlay removed his hat and slipped through the
trees. Slocum laid his sombrero over his saddle horn
and followed the marshal to the edge of the rimrock.
Both men lay on their stomachs and looked down into
the valley. They looked at the terrain with the gaze of
veteran manhunters.

Down below, the ghost town was an abandoned village holding a few dilapidated houses. A single rutted
street was lined on both sides with clapboard buildings.
The buildings looked decayed and untended.

A thin wisp of gray smoke drifted up from the chimney of one building, a two-story structure with a faded
sign painted on the front. The faded letters read PARA-
DISE VALLEY HOTEL. The ramshackle building appeared

to be the headquarters for the Ramey gang.

The sides of the buildings in the town were thrown together from unpainted ripsawed lumber. Their roofs were either planks coated with creosote or tin sheeting. A creek flowed through the valley, running alongside the street and buildings. The creek was lined with cottonwoods and willow trees. A corral contained about eighteen horses, two mules, and a small burro. The corral was near the hotel.

Findlay grunted and pointed his finger toward the corral. "Do those horses look familiar?" he asked.

Slocum pointed out the big stallion, which the moon-faced kid had grabbed coming out of the bank in Cheyenne. The brown and gray pinto was munching grass in a corner of the corral. "They're the same," he told Findlay.

"They're there all right," Findlay whispered. "The whore was telling the truth. You never know about women of the night. Some of those fallen angels will do anything to sell their charms. Some of them drink a lot of booze. The alcohol fuzzes their brains, and they get to imagining things and conjuring up fancy lies. That's why I wanted you along, Slocum. You're the only person who can identify the bandits and their horses."

"Do they get a chance to surrender?" Slocum asked.

"Sure. I always give a man that chance," Findlay said. "The whole bunch can spend the rest of their lives in the Detroit House of Correction. I don't think the Ramey gang is smart enough to surrender."

"And if they're not?"

Findlay jerked his head back toward the horses. "That's why I brought those two boys with us," he said. "They don't talk much. Neither of them is a show-boater. They're good shots with a rifle or revolver, and

they don't mind shooting to kill. Fact is, these two deputies like stopping a bunch like the Ramey gang."

"When do you plan on going in?"

Findlay looked up at the sun. "The gang probably drank
a lot of whiskey last night. They're sleeping it off. No use
in wasting time, my dad used to say. We'll go around the
rimrock, go down, and come up through the creek. The
trees will provide cover until we're right into town."

An hour later they rode through the creek a quarter mile
away from the town. Findlay raised his hand, and, as
silently as possible, the four men tied their horses to the
cottonwoods along the creek banks. Everyone checked
their carbines and nodded silently when Findlay handled
out extra cartridges. Each man received five extra boxes
of shells.

Then Findlay motioned with his hands and they
walked along the edge of the creek bank toward town.
When they arrived on the edge of town, everyone was
given whispered instructions. The two deputies slipped
away and took up positions on the back side of the
street. Findlay and Slocum took up a position facing the
front of the building.

Slocum left Findlay as the U.S. marshal slipped
through the back door of a one-story house. The man
from Georgia crept to the house beyond that and discovered the back door had been knocked loose from the top
hinge. Carefully, Slocum tiptoed his way inside.

The building was divided into two rooms. The back
room contained the bottom part of a cast-iron stove.
Slocum moved carefully past two rusting pieces of
stovepipe, then crept into the front room. The floor was
littered with a thick layer of dust. The only window in
the abandoned house was broken out of the small sill.

Slocum moved silently across the littered floor, crouched down, and took up a position. The only movement around the hotel was thin smoke rising from the stone chimney chinked with clay. Slocum checked his weapon, then eared back the hammer of his Winchester. The metallic snicking sound broke the silence.

Slocum waited for Findlay to make his move. The man from Georgia's thoughts went back to his service in the Confederate army during the Civil War. He thought about his baptism of fire under the command of General Thomas Jonathan Jackson.

A fiesty fighting spirit led to Slocum's promotion to sergeant and the command of a group of Confederate sharpshooters. Later, he had been the leader of a group of snipers who kept under cover and waited for a chance to fire upon Federal officers. At that time, during some of the hardest battles of the war, John Slocum learned the techniques of being a deadly sniper.

Now, fragmented memories of those wartime experiences flooded Slocum's mind. By some twisted fate, he had been chosen to come to this valley with J. J. Findlay and his two deputies. Slocum hoped the Ramey gang would surrender, that bloodshed would be avoided. But if the bandits decided to fight, Slocum would do his duty for the law.

Then Findlay decided the time had arrived to make his move.

The U.S. marshal squeezed off a round from his Winchester that sent a lead slug into the upstairs window of the hotel. Slocum watched the building for some sign of activity. Several minutes passed before a man's face appeared at the window. He rubbed sleep from his eyes and looked down into the ghost town street.

"Hello, the hotel!" Findlay shouted.

The man's face vanished back into the darkness of the hotel.

"This is the United States marshal," yelled Findlay. "You're surrounded by a large group of men. You got two minutes to come out with your hands held high above your head."

A guttural yell came from the building. "Go to hell, you bastard!"

A rifle barrel smashed the window of another room in the abandoned hotel.

"You don't have a chance!" Findlay yelled.

The rifle exploded and a bullet chunked into the building Findlay occupied.

After that, the lawman stopped talking. He took aim with his Winchester and pumped two bullets into the window where the rifle had been. Simultaneously, the two deputies shouldered their rifles and pumped several rounds into the building. The crack of the carbines sounded like a booming tattoo in the afternoon air.

Slocum did not waste lead. His work as a sniper had taught him to have patience. The deputies had the back entrance of the building in their line of fire. Anyone coming out the back door of the hotel would face their guns. Coming out the front entrance would put them up against the Winchesters manned by Findlay and Slocum.

Suddenly, the front door of the hotel was flung open. A lanky man wearing denim shirt and pants came running out of the building. He raced across the porch, firing wildly as Slocum took aim at him. Slocum squeezed off a round. The sharp crack of the rifle echoed in the room.

Slocum's slug smashed into the back of the bandit's knee. The man went tumbling off the porch as his leg gave way. He rolled into the street with blood gushing from his leg. He lay sprawled there for an instant, then, with some inhuman strength, clawed the earth and stood up. He still held the revolver in his hand.

Now, eyes wild, his face tightened with rage, the bandit looked for a target. Both Slocum and Findlay's Winchesters exploded. The deafening volley sent two slugs smashing into the man's midsection. He was jolted back against the steps of the porch, blood spurting from his stomach and shoulder. The bandit gave a feeble wave of his arm, then fell back with his head at an awkward angle.

Suddenly the ghost town was filled with the booming roar of guns. A beehive of lead swarmed out of the building toward Slocum's building. Bullets chunked into the timbers and sides of the house. The windows of the hotel seemed to be a wall of flame as the bandits fired through them.

Slocum grunted, dropped low, and crawled toward the back of the house. Lead poured into the window opening as he moved back into the kitchen area. He stood erect, kicked a dusty piece of stovepipe aside, and hurried out the back door.

Outside, he waited until the firing lessened, then raced to the building where Findlay was holed up.

"Slocum back here," he cried, going into the back of the house.

"You all right?" asked Findlay, who was watching the hotel through a paneless window.

The house was one large room. A battered chest of drawers was overturned against a wall. A horsehair sofa covered with dust was pushed against the opposite wall. One of the sofa's cushions had been removed and partially burned. The floor was charred with the blackened evidence of some past fire.

"It was getting mighty uncomfortable over there," Slocum said. "What's happening out there?"

"They're thinking," grunted Findlay. "The corpse in front of the hotel has got them spooked."

Slocum took a quick look outside. The windows of the hotel were empty.

"I think they're checking out the back way," Findlay said.

The marshal had barely finished his sentence when gunfire exploded in the back of the hotel. This was followed by the sharp crack of the deputies' rifles. Someone howled in the hotel. The cry was followed by loud, profane cursing.

Findlay leaned forward. He shouted out the window, "Give up, Ramey. You don't want to die!"

The hotel was quiet for the next ten minutes. Slocum and Findlay strained to hear any movement. The bandit gang had stopped fighting for the moment and were most likely discussing the possibility of surrender. Either that, Slocum decided, or they had escaped from the building by some secret entrance unknown to the lawmen.

Slocum remained tense, his gaze fastened on the front of the building. More time passed. At last Slocum said, "I hope you're a patient man, Findlay. We can sit here a long time. Ramey's bunch probably has food and water in the building. They may be trying a waiting game."

Findlay looked grim. "We can always wait until night falls and set fire to the building."

"You want to wait?" Slocum asked.

"Naw, I don't have the patience."

"What are your plans?"

"I'm thinking, man," snapped Findlay. "Don't push. You got any ideas?"

"We might start by making sure the horses in that corral are turned loose."

"You think they're planning to run for it?"

"Would you want out of here if you were in their spot?"

"Reckon I would," Findlay answered.

Then the gunfire from the hotel started up again. Another swarm of lead was directed at the building where Slocum and Findlay were settled in. More gunfire sounded from the back of the building. Slocum kept his eyes on the windows in the hotel, but the bandits were elusive: they stayed back from the windows and fired their guns without aiming at a specific target.

Slocum walked to the back of the room and looked around at the piles of junk scattered there. He picked up a large piece of wood, went back to the front of the room, and knocked a plank loose in the front wall. This provided a vantage point to keep an eye on the hotel.

He had barely started his surveillance when he saw something move across the street. A bandit had slipped through a side window and flattened himself against the building. Then the robber vanished from sight.

The gunfire from the hotel slacked off.

Slocum informed the marshal that one or more of the bandits were out of the hotel. "They may be making a move," Slocum said.

"Like what?" Findlay kept his gaze on the hotel.

"Slipping around to get us or your deputies."

Findlay shook his head. "Vermin like Ramey don't have the courage," he replied.

Slocum disagreed. "Men will do a lot of things to save their lives."

Suddenly the sound of revolver fire came from the other side of the building.

"They got Jesse," someone yelled.

Findlay cursed.

"Who's Jesse?" asked Slocum.

"One of my deputies."

Slocum's senses became sharp. He looked at Findlay with a wondering expression. "How many horses were in the corral?" he asked.

"At least a dozen."

"We've been dummies," Slocum said. "You figured Ramey's five men were the only ones here. Hell, Findlay, we may be facing half the outlaws in Wyoming."

Findlay started to reply, but his answer was cut short.

The back door of the building was kicked open.

Slocum made a dive behind the horsehair sofa.

A barrage of bullets came whizzing into the room.

4

The back side of the room turned into a wall of exploding flame.

Slocum rolled behind the horsehair sofa. Two bullets smashed into the thick upholstered side. More lead slammed against the plank walls behind the sofa.

J. J. Findlay let loose a sharp yell. A lead slug had slammed into the marshal's body. Findlay tried to get up, but the bullet had smashed the muscles of his right leg. Blood spurted out of the bullet hole and down the leg of the marshal's trousers. Findlay made a low, murmuring sound and fell back against the wall.

Slocum tensed for the impact of another bullet. He heard someone laugh.

The moon-faced youngster walked into the room. He held Colt revolvers in his hands. The kid looked at Findlay, who had dropped his gun when he was hit in the leg by the bullet. The marshal was trying to retrieve the weapon.

"Quit trying to get that gun," snapped the kid. "I

don't reckon on killing ye, lessen you try to kill me. You, behind the sofa"—the kid kicked the front of the battered horsehair couch—"throw out your guns, 'cause I wanna get away without buckshot in my back."

Slocum hesitated.

"Threw 'er out!" The kid's voice whipped through the room like the crack of a blacksnake whip.

Slocum threw out the Winchester rifle. The weapon clunked on the dirty floor in front of the sofa.

"Pistols, too," said the kid.

Slocum hesitated again. He didn't want to be without a weapon if the kid decided to kill two defenseless men. Sighing, Slocum threw out one of his revolvers. He stood up with his hands raised high above his shoulders.

"By golly!" The kid looked pleased. "You're the gent who give me a break in Cheyenne. You could have kilt me. Ye must be a purty good feller."

"Reckon so," Slocum drawled.

"What the hell is this?" demanded Findlay. "A gun-man's reunion?"

The kid looked over the barrels of his twin pistols. "Hold yore tongue, mister. You gents gotta promise to lay low till the gang gets out of here."

"Okay," said Slocum.

"Me too," added Findlay.

"Reckon I'll take yer word." The kid faced them, backing out of the room. "I don't figger stealin' ever hurt many folks. I don't like killin' people. I'll tell the gang that you're dead. Nobody's gonna check ye out, 'cause they're anxious to git out of here. Stay low and don't make any noise. We'll be goin' in a little while."

The kid wheeled on the heel of his boot and hurried toward the back of the house. The back door slammed, and the crunching of boots sounded on the ground out-side.

Slocum waited for a moment, then peered from be-hind the sofa. "You all right?" he whispered to Findlay.

"I ain't up to no all-day picnics with preaching on the grounds," said Findlay.

Slocum crawled over and pulled up the bloody leg of the marshal's trousers.

"What's it look like?" asked Findlay.

"Bone's been smashed up." Slocum took off his shirt, tore a piece of fabric from the garment and started to bind the marshal's wound.

Findlay's face was white with shock. "Ouch!" he winced. "Be careful down there. This is the first time I've ever been shot."

"You're lucky."

"I got some doubts about that. Maybe we're both lucky."

"How do you figure that? You're the one who got shot."

"That kid doesn't like killing people," answered Findlay. "Now, what's going on outside?"

Slocum remained back in the shadows but took a chance and looked outside. The street outside the hotel was filling up with a dozen men, who carried a wide variety of weapons. "They're having some fun," he told Findlay.

"You see either one of my deputies out there?"

"No sign."

"They must've got Jess."

"What's the other man's name?"

"George. Big George MacKay. He's probably gone. George would never stop fighting until he was dead.

Especially against vermin like this." Findlay swore
again.

"Keep quiet. Don't make any noise," Slocum hissed
in a low whisper. "You rouse these hardcases and we're
both dead."

Slocum sneaked another glance out of the window.
Some of the outlaws were running toward the corral.
More men came out of the hotel. They were laughing
and shouting, slapping each other on the back. They
were like prankish boys who had pulled a fast trick on
their parents or teachers. They were celebrating living
through the firefight.

Slocum stayed down; he heard the voice of the old
man yelling about stupid lawmen.

Amid shouts and laughter, Bart Ramey and his
friends saddled the horses. They went in and out of the
hotel, filling up saddlebags with supplies. Slocum
slipped over to the window, making sure he kept his
face in the shadows. He looked out into the street.

A dozen men were gathered in front of the hotel.
They looked like outcasts, a gang of reckless men with
a brutal attitude toward the world and everyone in it.

A man was standing on the front porch of the hotel.
Neither the man, nor the other members of the gang,
paid any attention to the dead bandit's body slumped
against the porch steps. Slocum watched the man who
seemed to be in charge of the activities. Slocum decided
the unimposing man was Bart Ramey, the bandit leader.
If Ramey had been riding the owlhoot trail for as long as
Findlay claimed, he was a good leader. He had proven
to be as slippery as a cornered otter, as deadly as a
riled-up grizzly bear.

Bart Ramey was the lean, thin man that Slocum had
seen in front of the Cheyenne bank during the robbery.

Ramey's scarred face was covered with the leathery skin of someone who has lived in the outdoors. His face was stringy, skeletal in appearance, and his lips were thin, almost bloodless. He was talking to the bandits now, giving their orders for the next few days.

"I want you to split up into bunches of three or four riders for the trip north into Deadwood Gulch," Bart Ramey said. "We got a better chance traveling in bunches. Eleven men traveling together will draw a lot of attention. But a few riders don't bring much interest from anybody. Anyone asks, you're going up to Deadwood to get in on the gold rush. You're tired of being a drover for cattle. You plan on making your fortune finding gold. You got that?"

"Yeah," someone yelled.

"Where do we meet up there?" asked another man.

"It ain't that big a place," said Ramey. "Not nearly as big as Cheyenne. Just drift into town when you get there. Act like you're interested in looking for gold. Try and blend in with the other people. If you're planning on drinking, keep your mouth shut and don't talk out of turn. Any questions?"

"Why're we leaving here?" The bandit's voice was thin, high-pitched.

"We just had a shoot-out with the U.S. marshal," Ramey replied.

"But we won," said the thin voice.

A couple of men whooped in celebration.

"Quiet down. There isn't any need to holler," Ramey snapped. He looked over at the bandit who had asked the question. "You asked why we're leaving here. I admit this is a good hideout. But we killed that marshal and his three friends. We killed four lawmen, and they're not those mealymouthed small-town marshals.

We left that sheriff dead in the streets of Cheyenne. Uncle Sam doesn't like his hired guns pushing up daisies. There are going to be a lot of people looking for us. We're sitting ducks out here. This is a known robbers' roost. Staying here marks us as outlaws."

"For dang sure," someone said.

Ramey went on, "Those four men come in here looking for us. Questions are going to be asked when they don't get back to Cheyenne. There'll be a posse coming after whoever pumped lead into them. Now, everyone have enough food and money? You should have your full share of the money and enough food for the ride to Deadwood."

The members of the gang nodded or voiced their agreement.

"I'll see you in Deadwood," Ramey promised.

Slocum watched as the bandit leader stepped off the porch, swung up into the saddle of his horse, and started off down the street. The rest of the gang followed Bart Ramey, who rode to the end of the rutted street. There the gang broke up into small groups. The gang was soon riding up the sloping ground to a pass out of the valley.

"They're gone," Slocum said at last. "Now we'd better look at that wound of yours."

"I'm not going to die," Findlay replied.

"Maybe not," Slocum agreed. "But you'll bleed to death in a few hours if we don't get you bandaged up. Come on, I'll help you stand up and we'll find someplace better than this to wash up your leg."

Slocum helped Findlay out of the dilapidated house, across the street, and through the front door of the hotel. Findlay sat down in a rocking chair and waited until Slocum cleaned up a bedroom on the ground floor. Then the man from Georgia went through the hotel hunting for a pair of clean sheets. At last, in a chest of drawers behind the check-in counter, Slocum found two worn satin sheets that were cleaner than the other bedclothes. He made the bed, then helped Findlay hobble out of the lobby into the bedroom.

Findlay stretched out on the bed. His face was white, and he bit his lower lip to press back the painful throbbing of his leg.

Slocum pulled his knife from his pocket. He snapped open the sharp blade and cut away the leg of Findlay's trousers. He threw the bloody fabric through the bare open window.

He came back and studied the wound. Bone and flesh were smashed into a bloody mess just below the marshal's knee.

While Slocum was inspecting the wound, Findlay raised up on his elbows and looked down. "Lordy," he said in a quiet voice. "I'll be lucky to ever walk again."

"Worry about that later," Slocum told the marshal. "Right now, we got to clean your leg to stop infection."

"Please check on my deputies first," pleaded Findlay.

Slocum went to the back of the hotel, went outside, and walked around. He found one deputy face-down in a thicket of tall weeds. The other deputy was slumped over behind an outhouse, half of his face blown away from a shotgun blast. Both men were dead. Slocum found a couple of tarps in the barn and covered their bodies.

Slocum was too busy to think in the next half hour. He took an iron poker and stabbed at the embers in the big iron stove in the hotel's kitchen. He added firewood and got a blaze going; then he carried two buckets to the creek and filled them with water.

When the water was boiling, Slocum went into the

bedroom and washed the blood, loose flesh, and bone from the marshal's leg. Then he bound the wound with strips of cloth from his shirt.

While the marshal was resting, Slocum went back to the creek. He walked through the knee-high weeds to where the pack mules and saddled horses had been tied to the trees. Although the animals were skittish, Slocum tied them with ropes and harness and led them into the ghost town.

He removed the saddles from two horses and hobbled them on one side of the hotel, out of sight from the direction the bandits had gone. The rest of the animals were turned loose in the corral. Before he went back into the hotel, Slocum fed the animals with a ration of grain and carried several armloads of fodder from a nearby barn.

He went inside the hotel and checked on Findlay. The marshal was sleeping; the leg wound had stopped bleeding. Slocum did not awaken the marshal, but tiptoed out of the building and checked the terrain around the ghost town. There was a peaceful atmosphere in Paradise Valley and, to a passing rider, no sign that a gunfight had occurred earlier that day.

Slocum rummaged through their provision bags, found several tin cans of food, and set about making a stew. Then he went outside and dug graves for the two deputies and the dead bandit. All three of the dead men were starting to bloat.

Slocum was happy to put them away in the shallow graves, away from the wild animals that would desecrate their corpses. He marked each grave with a fresh-cut stake and then went back into the hotel.

During the next two days and nights, Slocum nursed Findlay. The U.S. marshal was not an ideal patient. He refused to believe that the bullet wound would cause him to limp, that he might walk only with the aid of a cane. Findlay tried to stand up several times and, on two occasions, damaged his leg wound by trying to walk.

Slocum put up with the marshal's surly attitude. They argued whenever Findlay's wound had to be cleaned and bandaged. Slocum worried about gangrene and, on the second morning, awoke to find the marshal feverish and out of his head.

Findlay moaned, mumbled, and went on about hidden riches and gold strikes. Slocum figured the marshal was out of his mind. But, all that day and most of the night, Findlay ranted on about gold nuggets the size of hens' eggs.

Awakening on the third morning, the marshal was past the critical point. The fever seemed to have burned out the infection in his body. His mood was cheerful, his eyes unclouded, and his appetite was strong. Slocum prepared breakfast and went back to the iron stove again to fix another stack of pancakes for the ailing man.

When he finished the last bite of his second helping, Findlay raised up on his elbows on the bed. "I must have been out of my head," the marshal said.

"Yeah. You raved a lot."

"What about?"

"Mostly crazy stuff. Gibberish."

Findlay chuckled. "Well, I appreciate your helping me."

"That's the way a person should be."

"I might have died if you'd decided to take off."

"You'll get a chance to return the favor someday."

"Not likely." Findlay's expression darkened. "This leg will never be right. My days of knocking around the countryside are over."

Slocum realized that Findlay wanted to talk. The man from Georgia went to the side of the bedroom and grabbed a kitchen chair with a cane bottom. He turned the chair's back toward the bed and rested his elbows on the top of the chair.

"This isn't the end of the world for you," Slocum said. "I know plenty of men who have been injured. They make do with what they have left. Once, down in Arizona, I ran into a one-armed man who could outdraw either of us. One of the fastest gunfighters I ever met."

"You're saying that to make me feel good."

"Naw, he was called One-Armed Bob Baker. He was fast."

"A U.S. marshal has to be in good shape."

"True," Slocum agreed. "But there are other things you can do."

"Like settle down and be a good citizen."

Slocum shrugged. "Whatever you want to do."

"I'd like to own a farm. A nice place. Something like my folks had back in Pennsylvania."

"You could do that all right."

Findlay laughed. "I don't have any money."

"You were going on about some hidden gold last night."

The open expression on Findlay's face vanished. "Did I say much about it?"

"Naw. It was just a sick man's ravings."

Findlay frowned. "Did I talk about where it was hidden?"

"Nope. Besides, I wasn't paying too much attention."

Findlay's eyes narrowed. "Or maybe you wrote it all down."

Slocum bristled. "What is that supposed to mean?"

"Some people might move in on a crippled man like me."

"They might," Slocum agreed

"Listen to his comments and go get the gold for themselves."

"You believe that?" Slocum looked at the marshal with an expression of wonderment.

"Naw, I guess not," said Findlay. "You're still here."

"Don't get crazy on me."

Findlay forced a mirthless chuckle. "My mind isn't right."

"I can see that for myself."

"I'm more suspicious than I used to be."

"Well, I was just staying here to tend to you," said Slocum.

"I appreciate it."

"Then let's not hear any more about me taking your gold. After all, you asked me to come along." Slocum's eyes were hard. "I was good enough to be shot at."

"That's true."

"So I ought to be trustworthy enough to listen to your ranting and raving."

"What did I say?" Findlay asked.

"Something about nuggets the size of goose eggs."

"Anything else?"

"That the gold was hidden."

"It is."

Slocum stood up. "Look, Findlay, I don't want to keep talking about it. You talked about some big nuggets that were hidden. I don't know where you hid them, or if they exist. I figured you were just talking out of your head. Right now I have to feed the horses, make sure they're okay. Then we have to get you back to Cheyenne."

Findlay dropped his head back on the pillow. "You're sure I didn't say where the gold is?"

Slocum shook his head. "Nothing I heard."

"The gold is there, Slocum."

"Good. Go get it when you get well."

"You're not interested?" Findlay raised his eyebrows.

Slocum shrugged. "I've heard tall tales about gold since I came west. Most of them are pipe dreams."

"Why aren't you interested in money?"

"I like doing what I want to do."

"You can do it better with money."

Slocum shook his head. "Most people don't."

"What does that mean?"

"People get a little money and they get greedy."

"That's human nature."

"They start worrying about their money," Slocum explained. "They buy things and then get the worries about having them stolen. Things don't make you free. The less you own, Findlay, the more freedom you have. The more you own, the less freedom you have. If it doesn't fit in a saddlebag, I don't want to own it."

"Money is a way of keeping score," Findlay interjected.

"Of what?"

"The game of life. It separates the winners from the losers."

Slocum snorted derisively. "Life isn't a game. And I don't put labels on people."

"You know what I mean."

"Maybe I do," Slocum said. "I got to tend to the animals. You need some rest. We'll talk later."

5

J. J. Findlay was able to travel after two more days of rest. He was still hurting, but he thought the pain was something he could bear. There was a sharp, intense pain when the U.S. marshal hobbled out of the abandoned hotel, holding himself upright with a crude crutch fashioned out of a cottonwood limb. Findlay gritted his teeth and let Slocum help him up into the saddle.

A trail out of Paradise Valley led west across the isolated country to connect with the Cheyenne-to-Deadwood road. A stagecoach station was located there. The station allowed passengers on the stagecoach to rest and eat while the tired horses were replaced with new animals.

Slocum and Findlay rode off in that direction. They had saddled two of the horses, a big dun for Findlay and a big black stallion for Slocum. Then they roped the remaining horses and mules together to create a long line of single-file animals.

They left the burro untied, but he romped along happily after the horses and mules. Sometimes the burro would wander off the trail to feast on a patch of weeds or grass. But just when the men and animals started to vanish, the little donkey brayed and raced to catch up.

Both men kept a wary watch on the surrounding terrain for bandits, unknown riders, or war parties from the Indian tribes. The western tribes were on the warpath. They had been shoved back away from the good hunting grounds. White miners and ranchers were moving in to claim tribal lands. The Indians retaliated by riding out on war parties that killed any whites in their area.

Findlay was silent for most of the morning. He sat in the saddle on the big dun, immersed in his thoughts. They seemed to be coming to him in bits and pieces. He couldn't make out exactly what it was his mind was chewing on. Ideas formed and then seemed to evaporate like the fog off a creek drifting up to die in the morning sun.

His mind got so jumbled up that he became dizzy. He swayed in the saddle and thought he would fall off the horse, but Slocum saw his body weave on the big horse, dropped back, and suggested they stop and rest for a spell. They were on flat ground now, riding alongside a small creek that ran muddy from rain up in the country.

Findlay laughed at his dizziness, though he thought he might be going crazy. But he reined in his animal and allowed Slocum to help him down to the ground. The pain in his leg was intense and burning, but he bit his lower lip and hobbled across the meadow and sat down on a large boulder. He fought with the pain and pushed it down. He had shot a lot of men, shot fast and quick without wondering how it felt to have a lead slug tear into flesh and bone.

Now, J. J. Findlay knew the pain of a gunshot

wound. He felt as if he could hear the bones in his legs scraping together, mashing down hard on top of each other, an abrasive grinding that would never end. He sat there on the cold rock and wondered if he would ever find the courage to shoot another man. He bent over and took his painful leg in both hands, trying to squeeze out the pain.

Slocum watered the horses, making sure they didn't drink too much and get bloated. Then he came over and hunkered down beside Findlay. Slocum kept a close watch as the animals grazed along the edge of the creek. "You feeling any better?" he asked.

A wracking groan came out of Findlay's mouth. "Lord, Slocum, I'm going through something I don't understand."

"Want to talk about it?"

"I don't know," Findlay answered. "It isn't something I can put into words. Right now, my mind is playing tricks with me."

"What about?"

"My days of hunting down outlaws are over." Findlay's voice was like a thin whine. "I've lost my nerve. This bullet done me in."

"Ah, it isn't much," Slocum answered. "You get over the fear. It just takes a little time."

Despite the pain, Findlay smiled crookedly. "There isn't much call for a gimpy-legged lawman who's lost his courage. I might as well take that shotgun out of the scabbard and blow my brains out. I don't want to go through life sneaking around like a coward."

"I've been shot, knifed, and beaten up a few times," Slocum said. "You accept the fact that you may get hurt. Nobody gets a guarantee on a long life out here. You rest for a while and then we'll ride on out to the stagecoach station. Things will look better when we get you back to Cheyenne."

"I doubt it," Findlay said.

"Hell, it has to."

Findlay shook his head. "You said there were no guarantees."

"I guess so," Slocum agreed.

They rode on after resting for half an hour. Findlay's mind shifted and twisted until he whimpered with anxiety. Slocum rode close to the marshal, watched the lawman's movements. Once, when they came up on a crest in the trail, Slocum saw Findlay start to pull his revolver from his holster. Slocum rode close and took the gun from the lawman.

"I'll be better off dead," snapped Findlay. He made a grab for the shotgun in his scabbard.

Slocum also took that weapon. He was beginning to look forward to getting Findlay back to town.

Findlay looked up into the afternoon sky. The sun was hot, an angry ball of fire that baked the world with heat.

They stopped early and made camp beside a small stream. Slocum watered and fed the horses while Findlay sat beside the creek and stared off into the distance. The lawman looked at the world with a sense of desolation. He wanted to dig a big hole and crawl into it, or find a cave that was warm and dry as refuge against the outlaws, gunmen, and hardcases. A haven where men who lived by the gun could not find him. He raised his hand before his drawn face and watched the nervous trembling as he shook with fear.

After eating a dinner of trout caught by Slocum from the stream, Findlay's condition seemed to improve. He stretched out beside the campfire as the sun lowered in the west. Findlay spoke in a calm, measured manner. "We'll be at the stagecoach station by noon tomorrow. A daily stagecoach goes down to Cheyenne. You can drop me off there and I'll make it back alone."

"I'll go back with you," Slocum promised. "I've got nothing better to do."

Findlay shook his head. "I've got a better plan. Are you a gambling man?"

Slocum grinned. "I've been known to play a few hands of poker. But I'm not too flush right now."

"This won't require money."

Slocum raised his eyebrows and gazed at the lawman. He wondered what kind of scheme Findlay had thought up. "I'm listening," he said.

"Last January I arrested an old-timer named Elijah Tobias Thurston," Findlay went on. "Thurston was a hardcase. He come west early with some of the fur trapping expeditions coming north out of St. Louis. Later he fought in the Mexican War. Thurston wasn't the most ethical man around, so the war was an excuse for some top-grade looting, pillage, and plundering."

Slocum nodded. "Some soldiers favor that type of activity."

"One of the places that Thurston and his men hit was an old Spanish church down in Mexico. The place was almost the size of a cathedral. The Spaniards must have used it for their headquarters. Thurston's crew broke into the place and found a whole back room of the church piled high with old Spanish records. They didn't know how far back the records went. Most of the Americans couldn't read their own language, much less the Spanish used by the conquistadors."

Slocum decided to go along with Findlay's story.

"They found a treasure map," he said. "That has to be it."

Findlay looked disappointed. "That's exactly right. Have you ever seen one, Slocum?"

"By the bale."

A puzzled expression came over Findlay's face. "Treasure maps don't come in bales."

"They do in Mexico."

"I don't understand," Findlay said.

"Is this one on parchment or sheepskin?"

"Sheepskin."

"They make them down there," Slocum explained. "I was across the border some time ago. I was stuck in a small town down there because a bandit army and the government troops were fighting all around the countryside. I had to wait until the fighting died down before coming north."

"So how does that connect with my treasure map?" Findlay's tone was high and edged with anxiety.

"I stayed with a family who made treasure maps."

"Made them?" Findlay's words came spewing forth like hot coals. "What do you mean they made them? What are you talking about?"

"The family took sheepskin and a piece of steel," Slocum related. "They'd sit in front of a fire, heat the steel, and burn in a map on the sheepskin. Then, when they had a few dozen maps made up, the father went across the border and sold them to a saloonkeeper in El Paso. I presume the barkeep sold them to people traveling through town, or maybe he added a profit and resold them."

"These were fake maps?" asked Findlay. "That's fraud."

Slocum laughed. "An old man in Caldwell, Kansas,

made a good living selling these bogus treasure maps to railroaders. A new engineer or brakeman was always good for five bucks, or maybe even ten or twenty. That's a small price to pay for a map to lead you to a hidden Spanish treasure."

"My map isn't lost treasure." Findlay reached inside his shirt and came out with a piece of rolled-up sheepskin. "This map shows where a nice strike of gold is located."

"But it came from Mexico. Right?"

"The man said it did."

"The thing is probably fake."

"It can't be."

"Didn't you arrest him?" Slocum asked.

"Sure."

"Why would a hardcase do you a favor?"

Findlay shrugged. "He's doing life in prison. He gave it to me because I wasn't beating on him during the trip back to prison."

"So he rewards you with the map?"

"Something like that."

"More like a curse," Slocum said. "I've known men obsessed with treasure maps. They spend years looking for some will-o'-the-wisp buried treasure. They're always going to find that treasure over the next hill, or down in the next valley. Some men find hope for the future in believing in these treasure maps."

"Well, my prisoner was sincere." Findlay's statement was accompanied by a smug expression.

"Maybe the man meant well," Slocum agreed. "But he may have been deluded by his belief in the map."

"Thurston said he found the treasure," Findlay declared.

"He did? Then the map isn't any good."

"But he couldn't bring out the gold."

Slocum thought about that for a moment. "This has all of the earmarks."

"Of what?"

"Your standard treasure story."

"This one is true." Findlay's voice was harsh. "Just listen to me. We can get rich."

"I doubt it," grumbled Slocum.

"Just listen, okay?"

"All right. I'll listen."

Findlay explained that the old man Thurston had carried the map out of Mexico. "He didn't go off half-cocked about it," Findlay went on. "He wandered through the West. Naturally, he kept an eye on some part of the country that matched the treasure map. After thirty years, he ran across a place that matched the map."

Slocum became interested. "Go on."

"Thurston was up in the Black Hills. You know about that mountain range?"

"Up by Deadwood."

"And sacred land for the Sioux Indians. You ever been in there?"

"No."

"Anyway, Thurston found the exact spot. Are you interested in seeing the map?"

Slocum's interest was aroused. He went over and hunkered down as Findlay spread out the sheepskin map. Lines and symbols had been burned into the map by a hot piece of metal. Several Spanish words could be seen at the bottom of the skin.

"Looks old," said Slocum. "Maybe those fake map-makers found a way to age their skins."

"Lord, you're a real cynic," snapped Findlay. "Don't you believe in anything?"

"Not a helluva lot," Slocum admitted. "I used to believe in things, but it always got me in trouble. I always ended up busted, broke, or on foot out in the wilderness."

Findlay made a sweeping gesture over the map with his hand. "The key is right here," he said. His forefinger tapped the skin. "A lake. Just a small one beside this mountain that slopes down toward it. But a sheer rock cliff makes up the bottom of the mountain. Inside here"—he tapped the skin—"is this cave that looks like an eye. The gold is inside that cave."

"What kind of gold?"

"Thurston couldn't get inside the cave to find out," Findlay went on. "It could be a lot of gold mined and smelted down by the Spaniards. Or maybe the mountain contains a vein of good gold. Thurston thought it might be a natural deposit. Now, you can identify the lake because it is above a bowl-like valley. Another identification point is this waterfall at the side of the lake. That's what feeds it. Finally, you have this cave that looks like an eye."

Slocum stood up and walked back to his bedroll. "How high is the cave above the lake?"

"I don't know. Thurston figured a man would have to come in from the top," said Findlay. "Get a rope and shimmy down from the top. He said there was a ledge just below the cave entrance. Of course, Thurston didn't have much time to look."

"Why not?"

"A Sioux war party was after him," Findlay explained. "They didn't like white men coming into their sacred land. Thurston went in to do some trapping. He spent a winter in there and was coming out with his furs in the spring. One afternoon he came into terrain that looked like his map. He was sure that was it. But he didn't have much time because he was jumped by a war party."

"Why didn't he go back?"

"I arrested him."

"Where at?"

"Up on the Powder River."

"How'd you find him?"

"I'd been looking for him for a couple of years. He'd been down in St. Louis some time ago. He killed a man in a barroom brawl."

Slocum looked suspicious. "You don't hunt a man down for that."

"You do if the dead man is the son of a big-shot politician."

"That's bad news," Slocum agreed. "Where's Thurston now?"

"Serving life in the Detroit House of Correction."

"He tie any strings to the map?"

"Just one. Get him out of prison if I find the gold."

"How do you do that?"

"Whatever it takes. Maybe a lawyer or a jailbreak."

"Why tell me about this?" Slocum asked.

"I was planning to get it," said Findlay. "Take some time off from my marshaling job. Wander around in the Black Hills until I found the place. One way or another, get my mind satisfied as to whether the gold is there. Now, with this leg injury, I'll never be able to pack in there."

"Hire a couple of helpers," Slocum suggested.

"I want you to hunt it down."

"Me?" Slocum pretended to be surprised, although he had figured that was Findlay's intention. "I'm not a prospector. I wouldn't make a good agent for you."

"Why not?"

"I don't have any great faith that the gold exists."

"It does," said Findlay. "I know it does. It has to exist. I'm going to lose my job as marshal."

"Maybe you can stay on."

Findlay laughed, a harsh barking sound. "You don't understand, Slocum. I've lost my nerve. I'm a coward. Hell, everything is just pretense for me. Folks thought I was brave and sure of myself. I was just a coward pretending to be tough. The Ramey gang proved that. I was petrified when that moon-faced kid came walking in with those twin guns. I don't want to die from some outlaw's bullet. I need the gold to get back east, buy me a farm, marry a good woman, and settle down."

"Maybe what you say is true," Slocum responded. "Every man knows when the time comes to cash in his chips. I could mosey in there and look around, except I'm short on cash."

"I'll pay the expenses and work out some wages with you."

"What about the wages?"

"Thirty a month, plus half of the gold you bring in."

"When would you want me to start?"

"We split up tomorrow at the stagecoach station," Findlay said. "I'll go back to Cheyenne, draw pay for myself, and put in a voucher for you. Then I'll wait until a new marshal gets out here. When he comes, I'll get up into the Black Hills and meet you."

"Let me sleep on it."

"Plus, you get half of the gold," Findlay added. "You get your share right off the top."

"What's to stop me from taking it all?"

Findlay smiled. "You're an honest man."

Slocum slept lightly that night, keeping the guns close by his bedroll. The feverish craziness seemed to have left Findlay after their conversation about the gold. Once, when the silver moon was high in the night sky, Slocum was roused by the sound of someone moving in camp.

Slocum opened his eyes and caught sight of Findlay padding off into the bush. The man from Georgia waited a few minutes, wondering if Findlay was wandering off on some feverish mission. More than likely, the marshal was going out of camp to relieve himself as the result of a night call.

Slocum pretended to be asleep when Findlay came back to camp. The marshal did not go near the guns. Instead, he crawled back into his bedroll and went to sleep. Maybe, Slocum thought, the craziness is over.

6

They spotted the stagecoach station shortly before noon. They reined in their horses and looked down from a high hill that provided a sweeping view of the northern Wyoming terrain. The vista showed the rutted Cheyenne-to-Deadwood trail rolling through the valley from the south, past a reedy marshland and across a couple of small streams.

The stagecoach station had been set up on the north bank of the last winding creek. The main feature of the road station was a large corral containing about three dozen horses. The station building was a sturdy structure of logs and stone, with weathered and unpainted sides. The design would enable a road station agent to fight off Indians, bandits, and other attackers.

They spurred their horses and rode down the slope toward the station. Even from the distance, Slocum noticed that the wrangler working in the corral had caught sight of their approach. The man had stopped working, gone inside the building, and returned with a revolver holstered on his hip. For whatever reason, the man at the stagecoach station did not take any chances with strangers.

As they crossed the creek and came close to the station, Slocum looked over at Findlay. "Do you know these people?"

"No worries from here on in," answered the marshal. "The station is run by a Swede, Gene Olson. He's a burly guy with muscles like rock. I've seen him lift a small pony off the ground. He's been tending the station out here for three years. I believe Olson has faced every kind of emergency. That includes Indian attack, problems with renegades, and a couple of ranchers who resented the stage line going through the valley. Olson is a tough hombre."

"I hope he likes me," Slocum chuckled.

"Olson likes everyone. He's an easygoing person," Findlay went on. "He has a lonely job out here. It gets complicated because the Indians would like to add a few animals to their herds. Plus, he's had problems with robbery gangs in the past. You can go over to the far side of the meadow and find a half-dozen graves. Those are people who underestimated Mr. Olson's stamina to defend himself and his station."

"He sounds like a good man."

"Indeed." Findlay was in an expansive mood. The marshal's moodiness seemed to have vanished. Slocum had relaxed most of the morning because Findlay's self-destructive tendencies were gone. He was clearly happy to be returning to civilization. The marshal coughed lightly, then added, "Slocum, I'm going to need my shotgun and guns. Olson will ask questions if I ride in with an empty holster."

Slocum twisted in his saddle and reached back into

his saddlebags. He handed over the marshal's revolvers and gunbelt. "I figure you're feeling better," he said.

Findlay buckled on his weapons. "I am. I'm obligated to you for watching out for me. I was funny in the head back there."

"How's your leg?"

"Not bad," answered the marshal. "I won't be running any road races, no sir, never again. But I feel real happy now that you're going after the gold."

"I haven't said yes."

"But you will? Right?"

"I might as well."

Findlay broke into a big grin. "That's great, partner. We'll make our fortune, buy a big mansion, and sit on a porch with our feet propped up on the railings. We'll have a few servants running to bring us a mint julep every half hour. And, when the booze warms our bellies and starts a stirring in our loins, we'll have a couple of tender young brides to quench the fire when we get the hots."

Slocum laughed. "Whatever you say, Findlay. It's your fantasy. Imagine anything you like."

"Well, it could happen," Findlay said defensively. "I knew a gent down in Kansas who made enough money as a buffalo hunter to buy himself a nice mansion in Kansas City. All he does now is tend to his investments, which are in one-family houses, and collect the rent. That takes one day a month. The rest of the time he lolls around with this young woman he married."

Slocum laughed. "Old men always want young women. Why is that?"

"Maybe it's the other way around."

"The girls go after the old men?" Slocum cocked an eyebrow.

"Look at it this way. A young girl doesn't take up with just any older man. She always looks for one who is well-to-do. Maybe not the richest man in town, but comfortable. Now, an older man isn't going to pester a girl to death in bed. Once a week in bed and he's thrilled to death. More than that and the girl will wear him out."

"I've heard that's true," said Slocum.

Findlay went on. "The young bride has plenty of money to spend, and, you know, women do love to shop. Plus, she has a man who genuinely appreciates her beauty and company."

"For as long as it lasts."

"That's another of the secrets. The old man isn't going to live forever. One day he's going to croak with a heart attack or stroke. It's best if he goes quick from a heart attack. That way, his young bride doesn't have to waste time nursing him. When he dies, his young widow gets the house, the investments, and all the money. She can go out and find herself a real humdinger of a husband. That is, if she's careful about not getting involved with fortune hunters."

Slocum laughed. "Like herself?"

"Well, think about it. The old guy gets a pretty little filly. The young girl gets security and whatever wealth he leaves behind. That's a deal where everyone wins. And another thing, Slocum—we know that a lot of young women just don't have much worldly experience. Lots of families shelter their female young'uns. An older husband can overcome that drawback and put some sense into the gal's head."

"Well, you make it sound like a business deal."

Findlay chuckled. "Whether you realize it or not, mister, that is exactly what marriage is. Maybe not for the man, because he lets his gonads dictate his actions. But believe me, women are different. They're as calculating as a Philadelphia bookkeeper."

They were coming into the yard of the road station. Gene Olson, a muscular man in a work shirt and overalls, walked out of the corral to greet them.

"One thing," Findlay leaned over and whispered in Slocum's ear. "We'll be splitting up here. If we talk about the gold, I'd prefer to do it when Olson isn't around to hear."

"I'll follow your lead," Slocum said.

"Don't forget," warned Findlay.

A half hour later the three men were sitting on benches around a rough plank table. Gene Olson had informed them that there was trouble with the Indians, that a Sioux war party had been seen in the neighborhood of the road station during the past few days.

"I ain't caught sight of them myself," he related. "But folks say that Gray Wolf and a batch of his braves are on the warpath. They're supposed to have killed a couple of prospectors who were panning for gold about twenty miles from here."

"Have they hit the stagecoach?" asked Findlay.

"Somebody did a couple of days ago," Olson replied. "Up in Dead Woman Pass. Arrows started whizzing at the driver and guard. He didn't stop to find out who was after him. He just let the horses loose and came running in here with the team half dead. Terrible, I tell you, the way some of these drivers treat their animals."

Olson explained that two outlying ranches had been attacked by the Sioux. Many settlers were moving into town until the Indians were pushed back onto reservations.

"I can't blame the Sioux," Olson explained, standing

on the porch and looking out over the rolling hills. "The tribes keep getting pushed further back. The Indians sign treaties with the Great White Father, who turns around and immediately breaks his word. The tribes are promised food and supplies, but they're stolen by the bureaucrats and Indian agents. White men have killed off the buffalo, which was the Indian's great source of food. Out here, if your skin is red, you have a hard row to hoe."

Olson invited them inside the station and rustled up some antelope stew, pinto beans, fried potatoes, and sauerkraut. The victuals were washed down with large cups of milk cooled in a well beside the road station. And, for dessert, Olson brought out a warmed-up cast-iron pan containing blackberry cobbler covered with cream.

Gene Olson fixed everyone a large bowl of cobbler, sat across from them, and dug into the creamy dessert with a large spoon. He was a big, strong man—six foot two, two hundred and ten pounds, large-muscled—and he was a congenial person.

He was an honest man, Slocum decided, who didn't lie to his fellow men, wouldn't shortchange a customer, and gave more than he took in any trade. He was the type of man who didn't beat women, kick his hounds, or look for an easy way to get through life.

Olson had come west, so he said, after going broke in a general store in southern Kentucky. He wasn't interested in getting rich quick. He seemed to be content to run the road station, tend his garden, care for the horses, cook for the stagecoach passengers, and talk about the opportunity in the West.

After finishing their dessert, the three men walked

out onto the porch. They sat down and let the food settle after the large meal.

"I'm about ready to give up this job," Olson told them. "Too dang lonely out here. A man needs people around."

"Hire yourself a couple hands," said Findlay.

"Cost too much money."

"Get married to some nice gal," said Slocum.

"Can't find one."

"Run an advertisement for a wife in one of those eastern newspapers," suggested Findlay.

"I did."

"What happened?" Findlay asked.

"I got five replies from women back east. They sounded meaner than a rabid skunk. One lady wanted to make sure I wasn't interested in any of that bedroom stuff. Said she'd been almost wore out by her first husband, who kept rutting and pestering her in bed. Another one had seven young'uns and wanted a husband with a strong hand to keep the kids in line."

Slocum laughed, "She didn't need a husband. She wanted a sheriff."

Olson chuckled in agreement. "It would be a test of character going from being single to the daddy to seven kids. Lord!" He rolled his eyes. "That would try any man's patience."

"What about the other three women?" asked Findlay.

"One lady was bald," Olson went on. "Now, I'm not the sort to get all worked up about a little missing hair. Although, it does look good on a woman. A man, too, for that matter. But she swore she lost her hair after seeing a ghost. It must've been a terrible haunt. She got a nice wig, but someone stole it. Not only that, but she wanted me to send her fifty dollars for a new wig and another forty to buy one for her sister."

"Her sister was also bald?" This came from Findlay.

"Maybe they seen the same ghost," Olson explained. "I got the letter inside if you want to read it. Kinda pathetic, when you get to thinking about two bald-headed women waiting for me to send them their wig money."

The three men laughed.

"Mail order romance ain't much," said Olson. "Most of the women want money. One way or another, you're sending money to some strange woman back east. I'd rather go into town and play poker. At least you get to drink a few beers while someone bottom-deals the deck. You get some enjoyment, at least, and a few hours of conversation."

Olson excused himself, went back to the barn, and returned with a jug of blackberry wine. He went inside the station, picked up three tin cups, washed them, and came back out on the porch. Slowly and with great cere-mony he poured wine into the cups and passed them around. "To city life," he said, holding his cup up in a toast.

"Maybe not that radical," said Slocum. "Here's to people."

"Amen!" Findlay said, then took a sip of the wine, found it to his liking, and drained the cup.

They were starting on their second cup of wine when Slocum noticed a cloud of dust down the trail. He squinted through the late afternoon sun and caught the image of several covered wagons moving swiftly toward the road station. "We've got company coming," he said.

Olson looked toward the south. "A couple of wagons. Who the hell would that be?"

"Settlers?" Findlay asked.

"They'd have to be awful dumb," said Olson, "to leave Cheyenne with the tribes on a rampage."

"They're in a hurry," Slocum said. "No one in his right mind runs wagons at that speed."

"Whatever and whoever," Olson replied, "it looks like trouble. We might as well load up and make sure our shooting irons are ready."

The three men were waiting on the porch of the road station when the wagons pulled into the yard. The caravan consisted of two battered canvas-topped wagons pulled by sleek, grain-fed horses. The driver of the first wagon was a small, wiry man with steel-blue hair. The second rig had a middle-aged woman sitting on the wagon seat.

The driver of the lead wagon raised his hand in a gesture of greeting. "Howdy," he said to the three men on the porch. "I'm Dan Gunther."

"Glad to meet you, sir," Olson responded. "You folks were moving right along."

Gunther set the wheel brake and swung down from the wagon seat. "Indians," he said. "They came at us about an hour ago. Got our extra horses and a passel of mules, and a keg of whiskey we were taking to Deadwood."

"Anyone get hurt?" asked Slocum.

"We lost one man. I thought we'd run off the Indians, so we stopped to bury our friend. Barely got the grave dug when the redskins came back."

"They'll do that," said Slocum.

J. J. Findlay limped forward and introduced himself as the U.S. marshal.

Findlay's presence seemed to calm the man and the woman. Then the middle-aged woman snorted and asked where Findlay had been when the Indians were firing at her wagon.

"I can't be everywhere, ma'am," Findlay said. "And I've been wounded, as well. I suggest you get down from that seat, come inside, and get some rest. If there's a war party looking for horses, they may be thinking of hitting here. There's a lot of good horseflesh corraled out back."

"Yeah."

"Mamie, hop on down," Dan Gunther said loudly. "And tell those soiled doves of yours to come out from under that canvas."

"They're scared to death," Mamie declared. She wore an ankle-length black skirt, a white shirt-blouse, and a red scarf tied around her high slender neck. She wore too much white powder on her face—in an attempt to hide the wrinkles and age lines, Slocum figured: she was on the far side of forty years of age.

Slocum leaned against the front of the road station, chewing on a wooden toothpick. He watched as the middle-aged woman turned and said something into the back of her canvas-topped wagon.

A young woman with curly blond hair poked her head out of the wagon top. Then a splash of red silk flashed in the sunlight. A curvaceous young woman was standing in the road station yard, twisting a red and green parasol in her hands. "Hello, everybody," she said in a husky voice. "My name is Bunny."

"And I'm Trixie," piped in another woman. She shimmied down from the wagon and stood beside Bunny. Trixie was an auburn-haired woman about twenty-five years old, large-boned and almost six feet in height. She wore a dark blue suit with an ankle-length skirt, and a blue and white hat. A pearl pendant dangled from a gold chain around her neck.

"Well, Olson, ask and you shall receive," whispered Slocum.

"I'll be dad-burned," husked the road station keeper. "Praise Jehovah!"

"Wait up for me," came a cry from inside the wagon. Then a perky-faced young woman with a turned-up nose came into view. She was a petite person who was afraid to jump to the ground. Instead, she wailed about her dilemma until a red-faced Dan Gunther walked over and helped her to the ground.

"Are you all right, Miss Winters?" the blushing driver asked, stepping back and almost falling over his feet.

"Glory! You're just the sweetest person," gushed the girl. "You can call me Debbie."

"Thank ye kindly." The teamster tipped his fingers to the brim of his hat and hurried away.

Madam Mamie looked at her charges with a stern expression.

"I want you girls to exhibit your best manners," she announced. "We are going inside the road station to rest up. Remember, we are the guests of the Cheyenne-Deadwood Stagecoach Company. We will not be acting like trollops or soiled doves. We are going to be ladies."

"Yes, Miss Mamie," said Trixie.

"I'm always a lady," said Debbie.

"Does this mean we can't fiddle-faddle around?" asked Bunny.

"Hush," admonished Miss Mamie. She looked up at Olson, the station keeper. "Could you direct us to a place for our rest?"

"Huh?" The station keeper looked dumbfounded.

"The outhouse," whispered Slocum.

"Out in back, ma'am," Olson croaked.

"Perhaps we should make introductions," said Madam Mamie. "I'm Miss Mamie. Now, the girls have introduced themselves. What names do you high-class gentlemen go by?"

Slocum stepped forward a pace and introduced himself and his two friends. The women remarked on the wound in J. J. Findlay's leg and gushed over the fact that he was a U.S. marshal. When Gene Olson was introduced, they remarked about the cleanliness of the stagecoach station and the beauty of the surrounding area.

"Now we know each other. The girls and I will get cleaned up and refreshed, and we'll get better acquainted." With that, Miss Mamie picked up the hem of her skirt and led the three giggling girls along the porch and around the side of the house. As she sashayed past Slocum, Bunny looked up into his face. She winked one of her blue eyes and stuck out a half inch of pink tongue.

"Come on, Bunny," said Miss Mamie in a stern voice. "Don't dilly-dally with those fellows."

Slocum, Olson, and Findlay watched the women vanish around the side of the station. Olson had a big grin spread across his face. He shuffled his boots, looked down at his feet, and a low, chuckling sound came rushing up out of his throat.

"The cat sure hasn't got your tongue," remarked Slocum.

"Oh, dad-burn it! The Lord doth provide," giggled Olson. "I'm sitting around, drinking wine, and feeling bad because there ain't a woman in a fifty-mile radius.

Excepting Mrs. Kincaid over at the K-Bar Ranch. But she's all married up. And, quick as spit on a stove, along comes this wagon train carrying a whole passel of perfume-smelling women."

Slocum grinned. "And right behind them may be a Sioux war party looking for some female companionship."

"They won't be a problem," said Olson. "The thought of tumbling with one of those gals gives me strength. I could whip the whole Sioux nation right now. And you can add in the Blackfeet, the Cheyenne, the Arapahoe, and the Utes for good measure."

Out behind the stagecoach station, Madam Mamie took over the outhouse while her girls formed a line. They were giggling and discussing the Indian attack, the bravery or cowardice of the Indians, and the appearance of the three men at the station.

"That big federal marshal is divine," said Trixie. "I'd love to snuggle up to him in bed on a cold night."

"I like the station keeper. He seems so sincere," said Debbie. "I might even give him a freebie. I wonder if he has a woman out here."

Bunny laughed. "Men! Men! Men! Don't you girls ever think of anything else?"

"Sex! I think a lot about that," giggled Trixie.

"And men eating me," laughed Debbie. "Which one of those gents tickled your fancy, Bunny?"

"Why, all of them," Bunny answered.

"That's Bunny!" Trixie laughed. "Always ready to take on the whole world. Don't you ever get enough?"

Bunny shook her head negatively. "I like men and what they got betwixt their legs. It riles me to have to make a choice. One man over another ain't fair to a girl like me with big appetites. So I figure on just having all the men I can at one time or another."

"You're a greedy gal," hooted Debbie.

"I never horn in on your men," Bunny pointed out. "I don't poach another gal's mate."

"Not when I'm looking."

"Ain't Mamie ever going to get done in there?" Trixie wanted to know.

"We ought to plan something special for tonight," said Bunny.

"Like what?"

"Well, maybe give all the men a blow job," the girl replied. "I'll bet that's special out here where there ain't no women."

"Honey, that's special anywhere," said Debbie.

"We going to charge them?" asked Trixie.

A voice sounded inside the outhouse. It belonged to Madam Mamie. "You dang tooting we'll charge," the madam declared sternly.

7

The women returned to the front porch and were shown into the station by Gene Olson. They made gushing remarks about the interior of the station, which was clean and well maintained. They admired the gun holes bored into the walls, marveled at the furniture that was dust-free and well-oiled, and talked about "those nasty old Indians."

Findlay and Slocum remained on the front porch with the driver, Dan Gunther. Slocum wanted to know more about the Indian attack.

"Plain as could be," Gunther told him. "The trail goes through a small pass about five miles south of here. They were waiting on this side. The war party attacked after we passed through. For a moment there, I was really scared. They had a tree dropped over the trail. But I had room to change the direction of the wagon and skirt around it. Luckily, Madam Mamie is a pretty good teamster. She followed right behind me. That woman is a darn good driver."

"Were the Indians after the women?" Findlay asked.

"Maybe. More'n likely they wanted my load."

"Which is?" Slocum asked.

"I'm carrying repeating rifles and ammunition to Deadwood."

Both Slocum and Findlay were astonished.

"You got a wagonload of rifles and no escort?" Findlay's voice was a squeak of disbelief.

"That was Colonel Larchmount's idea. He's in charge of things down in Cheyenne," Gunther went on.

"I know him," said Findlay. He turned to Slocum. "His brain is as dense as a rock."

"He figured an Army escort would draw attention. But a couple of wagons would appear to be settlers," Gunther explained. "The colonel knew Madam Mamie was hankering to get to Deadwood. She'll make a lot of money up there with those good-looking girls of hers. Lord, if I wasn't a married man I'd be tempted myself."

Slocum laughed. "You've already been tempted."

"That's true," Gunther agreed. "But the thing is, I've kept my hands off those girls. Not that they haven't been willing to give a man a few favors. But I gave my vows to my bride, and that's the most holy promise I'll ever make. A man who would go back on his wedding vows can't be trusted. You couldn't take his word on anything if he broke his vows. They're the most serious promise a man ever makes."

"Thank God I'm single," said Slocum.

"Me too," added Findlay. "Besides, I used to know a jasper in Missouri who was scrupulous about keeping his marriage vows. He was a handsome cuss, too, and the women kept flinging themselves at him. But old George never paid them any heed. Just stayed pure and chaste. Right up to the day when he come home early and found his wife in bed with the Henson brothers, a couple of scurvy river rats with the morals of an alley cat."

"I trust my woman," Gunther pointed out.

"I'm not saying you don't have a good woman. She's as nice a person as a man will probably ever meet," the marshal replied. "Old George back in Missouri had that same feeling about his wife. I'm for grabbing the opportunity when it wiggles into view."

"What about that leg of yours?" asked Gunther.

"Where there is lust, me and one of those gals can find a way," said Findlay.

"More power to you," laughed Gunther.

"Don't let his words lead you astray," cautioned Slocum. "All of the old two-timers and bed-hoppers like Findlay want everyone to do it. Makes them feel better if everyone is sinning. Stick with what you think is best, Gunther."

"I will," the teamster promised.

That evening before supper, Gene Olson went into a back room. He returned with a fiddle and bow. He made a quick curtsy as the ladies clapped and began to call out their favorite tunes. Madam Mamie and Dan Gunther sat down on a bench while Olson played a lively tune.

Findlay was unable to dance because of his leg injury. That left John Slocum dancing around the floor with the three young women. He received immense enjoyment out of the company of the women. They were pretty, lively, and loved a good time.

Later, when Slocum and the women tired of dancing, the women pitched in to help prepare the evening meal. By now, Gene Olson had gone to the barn and rolled out a keg of wild cherry wine. The men dipped in with their cups and, between drinks, walked outside to check the countryside for any signs of Indians. The women claimed they were good cooks, that preparing a meal was fun.

"All we ever do is lay on our backs and get poked," declared Trixie. "Having men around to cook for is a real treat."

"You can get a permanent job right here," said Gene Olson, leering.

"I might take you up on that," said Trixie.

"He'd want some extras thrown in," Slocum remarked.

"Yeah, he's not thinking entirely of cooking," said Findlay.

"I am too," declared Olson, who was starting to slur his words. He had the flushed red face of a man who was getting drunk.

"Well, he'd get a little in that department, too," smiled Trixie. She did a hip-swinging walk across the room that brought whistles from the men.

"Come back here and stir these beans," said Madam Mamie in a tone of mock anger. "You'll get those men riled up until they're howling like wild animals. They'll be wanting the wrong kind of meat and we'll never get any supper."

Trixie exaggerated the wiggle of her hips as she walked back to the stove. "Men can be such babies," she declared. "They're so easy to please. All a girl has to do is lay back, take it easy, and they're happy."

"You've won my heart," declared Findlay.

"Give us a demonstration," yelled Gene Olson, who was starting to get drunk.

Trixie plopped a ladle into the bean pot and made a vigorous stirring motion. "What about you, Slocum?

You're awfully quiet. What's the key to your heart?"

"Long-legged women, fast horses, and good food," drawled the man from Georgia.

Trixie giggled. "And if you can't find a long-legged woman, you'll take one with medium or short legs. Right?"

"Something like that," Slocum agreed.

Everyone bantered and talked during the meal. The women were in good spirits. Slocum noted that their voices were a little too loud, their laughter a bit shrill. This was the result, he figured, of their escape from the Indian war party. They were recognizing the value of life after a dangerous experience.

Following the meal, Gene Olson went out to the barn and returned with another keg of wine. He set the cask on the table, which had been cleared by the women. Trixie and Bunny were off in the corner washing up the supper dishes.

"We might as well have a real party," Olson declared.

"I'm for that," agreed Madam Mamie.

"Me too," added Dan Gunther.

Olson looked over at Slocum, who was sitting at the end of the table. Slocum was fashioning a corral out of domino tiles.

"You want a few cups of wine?" Olson asked.

"Sure. What kind?"

"Wild grapes," Olson explained. "They grow all over the place around here. The whole countryside is covered with grapes when they're in season. Thick as fleas on a lazy dog. I mashed them with my own two feet."

"Did you wash them first?" asked Bunny.

"Naw. The grape juice cleans away the toe jam," laughed Olson.

"God! I'll bet you did that, too," Bunny responded.

When the room was cleared of dishes from the evening meal, they gathered around the table for some serious drinking. Gene Olson acted as host, passing out cups and jars of the rich, potent wine. Everyone drank eagerly, as if to erase their memories of past danger.

"So I come west to seek my fortune," said Trixie. She was sitting beside Dan Gunther and telling her life story. "I figured there wasn't going to be much going on back in Iowa. All you can find in Clinton—that's a sawmill town on the west bank of the Mississippi—is lumberjacks and drunks. Most of the time you find both of them in the same person. Clinton is a big sawmill town, you know, for handling the logs they cut up in Wisconsin and float downriver to the mills. A girl don't have no chance to find a good prospect for a husband. You know what I mean?"

"I think so," said Gunther.

"Lumber people drink like alcoholic fish," Trixie went on. "I thought of trying my luck in Davenport. That's a big town downriver from Clinton. But Davenport is full of Germans. All they want to do is drink beer, march in parades, and work."

"No loving?"

Trixie laughed. "Once a week, wham, bam, whether they need it or not. Germans pride themselves on being efficient. But you can be too efficient about some things, I always say."

"What kinda man you looking for?"

"One with two legs and a good-size dick," giggled Trixie. "That's not easy to find. Since I took up whoring for a living I discovered most men ain't very big where it counts. Six inches is hard to find, and eight inches is damned near impossible. I don't like measuring a man's worth by the size of his dong, but those big ones are the only kind that make me happy. I want to feel it knocking up there against my teeth when we do it."

Gunther said, "Lord, you talk dirty."

"I just tell the truth."

"My wife never talks about it."

"Hell, screwing is a natural thing," said Trixie. "Nothing to be ashamed about. Everybody does it, even mealymouthed women who pretend they never had a hand caress their privates. Not that I'm placing your wife in that category. What's your wife like? I'll bet she's a good woman."

"She's quiet."

"You got any kids?"

"A little girl. She's two years old."

"Don't let her grow up to be a chippy. Whores have a hard life."

"What's the worst thing ever happened to you?" Gunther asked.

Trixie was thoughtful, then got up and refilled their wine cups. She came back, sat down, and patted Dan Gunther on the knee. "The very worst? It happened to one of my customers. He'd been out surveying for a rancher. Been gone about two months and came back with a bad case of the hornies."

Gunther grinned. "I know the feeling."

"So he come up to my room and got undressed. Laid back on my bed while I was shedding my clothes. That's how you do it in a whorehouse, you know. Anyways, he had a giant erection. Claimed it was the biggest one he ever had. Something to write home about, maybe get a picture taken of it. You ever had one like that?"

"Maybe."

"So while I'm undressing, this nice old cat of mine is playing with a ball of twine. The cat was real nice, never hurt anyone. It was just playing around up on top of a chest of drawers that evening. Justin—that was my customer's name—was lying back admiring his big dong. Talking about it. Saying he would match it against anybody's in the whole world. He said I should go get a ruler and measure it so's we'd be able to tell everyone he was eighteen inches long. Hell, he wouldn't have made four inches with help from a Scotch rock."

"Justin must've been a bastard."

"Well, no, he was actually pretty sweet. He was just horny. Anyway, that cat caught sight of Justin's big one standing up in bed. The cat maybe thought it was a bald-headed mouse or something. Before you could say a word, that cat leaped off the chest of drawers. All four feet drawed back into claws. It zipped right through the air, landed smack dab with all four claws on top of Justin's pecker. And dug in with those claws."

"Oh, lord!" Gunther could almost feel the pain.

"The cat really dug into the head of Justin's prong," Trixie said with a giggle. "Then Justin started wilting. Real fast. So the cat thought he was attacking. The animal started scratching, spitting, and clawing at Justin's balls. Justin tried to knock it away, which made the cat mad, and it bit him on the shaft. Between the spitting, clawing, and biting, well—Justin was a mess. His big erection turned into a bloody, flaccid piece of flesh."

Gunther laughed. "I take it your friend was angry?"

Trixie rolled her eyes. She smiled. "Fit to be tied, as they say in Missouri. He come roaring up out of the bed with a painful expression. He wasn't your typical customer, that's for sure, because most are smiling when they get up. But old Justin didn't like my pussy cat. He grabbed for his gun, took two shots at the cat. The poor cat was hiding under the bed. Shooting up a cathouse will draw a lot of attention from the customers and the lawmen. One big guy come tearing into the room. He was naked as a jaybird, and he slapped Justin around for shooting up the place. The naked man claimed one of Justin's bullets went through the wall of the room and whizzed right past his head."

"Well, he had a right to be angry."

"Poor Justin went around soft as a dishrag for the next month," Trixie went on. "Plus, he was all black and blue from the beating that naked man gave him. This happened down in Dodge City. I didn't tell anybody, but word got out about Justin's fight with my cat. He was the laughingstock of the whole town. Everyone was funning at him. I felt real bad because he'd been a regular customer. That devil, Bat Masterson, offered Justin a hundred dollars if he'd do it again. Bat said he would sell tickets at a buck a head and make a fortune. So having Justin get his balls clawed was the worst thing that ever happened to me."

Gunther chuckled. "I'm sure Justin would agree. Did he ever come back to visit you?"

"That's the sad part," Trixie said. "He got the nickname of Claude Balls in Dodge City. People said he had authored a book called *The Cat's Revenge*. So Claude —I mean Justin—kept getting meaner and meaner. After the cat chewed him up, he was always fighting in saloons. That was because whenever he walked in some place, guys started laughing or snickering. Justin would get real touchy about it."

"Understandable," said Gunther.

"Finally, he left Dodge City and went to Colorado.

Dang, if he didn't run into a man from Dodge who knew all about the set-to with my cat. Wherever Justin went, folks say, he was followed by the cat story. I heard he was living like a hermit outside of San Francisco, raising vegetables and not talking to anybody."

"Strange things happen."

"Imagine a cat making all that fuss," said Trixie with a tone of wonderment in her voice.

"Justin was dumb," announced Madam Mamie. "All he had to do was be willing to laugh at himself. Then the whole thing would have been forgotten in a week."

"That's true," Slocum agreed.

Madam Mamie took a big swig from her wine cup. "But the little pissant kept getting riled up. He brought it all on himself with his rigid nature. Folks love to get your goat, especially if they know you're boiling inside."

Trixie's tale had caught the attention of everyone at the stagecoach station. Now it was Madam Mamie's turn to tell of her most bizarre experience. She took another sip of her grape wine, leaving a purple mustache on her upper lip.

"You gents have probably heard of snapping pussies," Madame Mamie said. "Happened to me when I was a young filly working in a busy house down in Natchez-under-the-Hill, Mississippi. Natchez was a proper, pretty town sitting on top of the bluff overlooking the river. Under-the-Hill was where the white trash, river rats, gamblers, bunco artists, and folks of that ilk hung out. Riverboats stopped over there to take on extra wood and to let off or take on passengers."

"What place did you work?" asked Bunny.

"At Aimee's House of All Nations."

Gene Olson asked, "You had a woman from every country?"

"Naw. It was just a way of drawing in the men," answered Madam Mamie. "Anyway, me'n' this gent were going at it one night. He was pretty good because I got real worked up. I was bouncing and twisting under him, really enjoying myself. Then my privates started making these spastic movements of their own accord. I didn't have any control over what it did. Then these spasms started getting bigger and stronger. Next, it was *ker-plunk*! One big snap and it stuck there."

"*Ker-plunk* would be right," Slocum remarked.

"My whole lower body was fastened around his manhood," laughed Madame Mamie. "He tried to pull out. No way. Then he started whining and whimpering because the *ker-plunk*ing was so tight he was hurting. You know, like taking your tool, putting it into a vise, and squeezing it shut."

"Lord, I don't even like to think about that," said Findlay.

"Me neither," added Slocum.

"Sounds kinda kinky," said Gene Olson.

"How'd you get untangled?" wondered Dan Gunther.

"We was stuck together like a couple of dogs," said Madam Mamie. "He got to yelling so loud that the owner of the house come in. Aimee was an old lady. She'd run cathouses all of her life. She knew what to do. She called a doctor, who come down and gave me some opium. That relaxed my muscles, and my poor customer was able to withdraw. He never got his rocks off, swore he wouldn't be able to use it for a week."

"That would be worse than Trixie's cat," said J. J. Findlay.

"How's that?" Slocum wanted to know.

"You can check a bedroom for cats, make sure they're not there," explained the marshal. "But a snapping pussy could attack you anytime."

"My wife could use some of that energy," said Dan Gunther.

"She's not good in bed?" asked Madam Mamie.

"Well, she ain't very helpful."

Trixie put her arm around Gunther's neck. "Poor boy!"

"She just lays there and never moves a muscle," said Gunther. "Like she's doing me a big favor letting me poke her. I could get as much action out of a dead woman."

"Dead woman?" Madam Mamie giggled. "Debbie, tell them about your first husband."

The petite young girl explained that she was born on a small homestead near Geneva, Nebraska. "It was grasshoppers, hot sun, and cold blizzards in the winter," she related. "I took off with a peddler to get away from Pa and my brothers. They were always grabbing at me, trying to pull me into the barn. I left the peddler in Omaha because he had the same ideas. I got a job as a roller in a cigar factory, barely making a living, when I went to church one night and met a real nice guy."

"What do you mean by roller in a cigar factory?" wondered Gene Olson.

"We took the leaves and rolled them into cigars," Debbie explained. "Anyway, this gent and I got to sparking pretty heavy and ended up getting married. He was an undertaker in a funeral home. We lived at the funeral home in an upstairs apartment. A nice guy. He just had one kinky bit. Before we went to bed he liked for me to take a real cold bath. As cold as I could get it.

Sometimes he would rub ice over my skin before we did it."

"Uh oh," said Findlay.

"One night I was in the apartment. My husband was downstairs getting a lady ready for burying. She was the daughter of a local banker. She'd been trampled when her buggy overturned and the horses ran away," Debbie went on. "I wondered what was keeping him down in the basement so long. So I went down to find out. There he was in the fixing room. He had the corpse all spread out and had mounted her. He was going at it, lickety split. The corpse had a mashed face where a horse had stepped on it. I was thunderstruck."

"Did you let him know you seen him?" asked Findlay.

"I pretended to be asleep when he come to bed," said Debbie. "The next morning I packed and left while services were being held for the banker's daughter."

"It takes all kinds," said Madam Mamie.

Dan Gunther hiccupped. "Yesiree! That undertaker would get along just fine with my wife."

"Poor baby!" Trixie caressed the back of Gunther's neck. "You ought to forget your vows and try riding a wild mustang."

Madam Mamie's face was flushed from drinking several cups of wine. "Tell them your story, Bunny," she laughed.

Bunny took a long swig from her cup of wine. "You mean that old thing about the fancy customer?"

"The man in Cheyenne," said Madam Mamie.

"Nothing much to tell," Bunny said, slurring her words. "He come in all horny and in a hurry. Dressed real fancy and didn't want to mess up his good looks by undressing. So I agreed to give him some oral satisfaction"—she rolled her eyes and grinned—"if you know what I mean. I was going along pretty good with him when, out of nowhere, I sneezed. It was one quick sneeze, but you'd have thought I bit right through it."

Everyone laughed.

"Maybe you did," said Gunther, putting his arm around Trixie's shoulders.

"Did he lose it?" asked Findlay

"Well, it wasn't much to begin with," Bunny said. "After I got done sneezing, you'd need a spyglass to find it."

"Lord, you girls have had some times," Findlay said.

"Mister marshal," slurred Madam Mamie. "I'll tell you the total and unvarnished naked truth. You never know what is going to happen when you're whoring for a living."

8

They continued to drink because the wine was good and the company was interesting. John Slocum ended up spreading his bedroll in a corner and snuggling in with Bunny for the night. Slocum's plans for sexual intimacy were interrupted when the young woman passed out, snoring lightly with a slack expression on her face.

Trixie and Dan Gunther wandered out into the night and were gone for almost an hour. Gunther came back inside the stagecoach station to refill their wine cups while Trixie waited in the doorway. Then, as they departed again, Slocum heard them crawling up into one of the wagons. Later, he heard the light noise of two bodies bouncing against the wagon bed.

Gene Olson had passed out early in the evening, face-down on the table. Madam Mamie, J. J. Findlay, and Debbie sprawled sideways over a cornshuck bed in the far corner of the room. Findlay was in the middle of the bed, both women snuggling close to him for warmth.

Dawn was rising in the east when Slocum felt a heavy hand on his shoulder. "Wake up!" hissed Dan Gunther.

Slocum roused himself. He shook his head to clear his mind. "What's wrong?" he inquired.

"Someone's prowling around outside," Gunther said. "I think that war party is back."

Slocum swore, stood up, and buckled on his gunbelt. "Where's Trixie?"

"Still asleep in the wagon."

"Better get her in here. Be quiet. Act as if everything is normal. You seen anyone?"

Gunther shook his head negatively. "Nope, but that makes me think it may be the Sioux."

"How many rifles you carrying?"

"Half a hundred," answered Gunther. "They're repeaters. Mostly Winchesters. A few Sharpses. Chrissakes! I should never have took this job. I should have known there would be problems if the Army didn't want to do it."

"How much ammunition are you carrying?"

"Maybe fifty boxes."

Slocum stood up. "We'd better get it moved inside. The Indians are probably after the guns."

"How could they have found out about them?" wondered Dan Gunther.

"I've never seen an Army post without a few Indians hanging around," said Slocum. "And the Army can get pretty loose-lipped talking about things."

"Yeah," said the teamster. "Half of Cheyenne knew I was bringing the guns up this way."

Dan Gunther went outside and came back in with a sleepy-eyed Trixie. She rubbed the sleep from her eyes, looked around for a minute, then lay down on Slocum's bedroll beside Bunny. Slocum went outside and carried in the guns and ammunition boxes handed down from the wagon by Gunther. They spent fifteen minutes getting the weapons inside the stagecoach station.

Their activity awakened Gene Olson, who helped stack the boxes inside the room. Their noise roused J. J. Findlay, who struggled out of the embraces of the two women. He hobbled over on his makeshift crutch and went outside into the yard. The marshal scanned the horizon for some sign of strangers. He stood leaning on his crutch and kept looking for some signs of a war party.

At last, Findlay was convinced the threat was a false alarm. "We've got excited for nothing," he announced. "The Sioux would hit right about dawn. The sun is too high for an attack. They're good at strategy, and the Sioux don't like losing men."

"That war party got a barrel of whiskey off me yesterday," said Gunther. "They may be sleeping off a bad hangover."

"Maybe," Findlay agreed. "Or, most likely, they're a day's ride from here. What do you think, Slocum?"

"We draw a keg of water from the well, post a lookout, and act as if they're out there," he said. "We're in luck if they're fifty miles away. We're prepared if Gunther is right."

"We can hold our own," said Gene Olson. "The walls have plenty of gun holes. We also got a couple of sniper holes up on the roof. You have to stand on a ladder, aim, and fire. And there's a couple of doors that lead out on the roof."

"Who thought of those?" asked Slocum.

"Mr. Henson, owner of the stage line."

"Sharp planning," said Slocum.

Olson agreed. "He figured they'd come in handy if a prowler went after the horses in the corral."

"Mr. Henson is a very smart man."

"Well, we can yammer inside," said Findlay, limping toward the door. "Time to wake up the women and have them make breakfast."

"Let them sleep," suggested Gene Olson. "I'll rustle up some grub."

"Go ahead," Slocum agreed. "You help him, Findlay. Gunther and I will fill the water troughs in the corral and make sure we have plenty of water to last a couple of days."

Slocum discovered that the clear, cool creek flowed through a portion of the corral. It was unnecessary to fill troughs for the animals. Instead, he and Dan Gunther filled two kegs of water and several water bags and carried them inside the building. Next they went out to the barn and brought in several kegs of Gene Olson's homemade wine and a barrel of white corn whiskey.

"We'd be in trouble if a war party got into this brew," said Slocum, rolling the whiskey keg into the station building.

Findlay leaned over and sniffed at the keg. "Hell, anybody would have problems with that stuff. It smells mighty potent."

"Got the kick of a mule," grinned Gene Olson. "My pride and joy."

Slocum discovered that the women had awakened and were getting up. They went to the outhouse behind the station. Slocum picked up his Winchester and went outside to stand guard. The last of the women had relieved herself when Slocum's eyes caught sight of the Indians. They were riding along the creek bank, heading upstream toward the stagecoach station. The war party rode rugged little ponies whose tails moved in agitated twitches.

The Indians sat tall and straight, with the ease of men who had been born to ride. They were smoky red, dark-eyed, and their hair was straight and black.

They moved with an arrogant calmness that was both natural and confident. Not one of those braves, Slocum thought, could ever think that anyone was his equal. They believed themselves to be lords of the earth, kings of the wilderness. The Sioux did not kowtow to the white man, nor hang around the forts and trading posts begging for trade goods and whiskey. A Sioux warrior was too prideful to beg.

Instead, the Sioux would lie back and wait for a breach in security. Then, racing in on their sturdy little ponies, they took what they wanted. Slocum knew they were not an evil tribe; their values were different from the ethics of the white culture. Indians believed in keeping their promises, while the government made treaties and immediately broke them.

That morning, the chief of the band rode a spotted black and white pony. His body was muscular, compact, and smeared with war paint. He carried a feathered lance in his arms. A bow and arrows were in a buffalo hide container tied with a strap around his pony's neck.

The Indians came forward at a steady pace. Slocum cautioned the women to get inside the building, then stood quietly as the Indians moved forward. They whooped as their ponies splashed through the water of the creek. One brave locked his legs around his pony, swung down beneath the animal, and scooped up a handful of water. His feat was applauded by the other warriors.

The chief led his riders across the creek, the hooves

of the ponies splashing in the water. Slocum gazed at the impassive faces staring at him. Their proud eyes were curious at the sight of the white man.

Then they stopped coming forward and veered their ponies out of the creek onto the opposite bank. They assembled in the meadow, leaped off their mounts, and talked. Occasionally one of the Sioux would glance across the stream and stare at Slocum.

Gene Olson came out of the station house. "What are they up to?" asked the station keeper.

"They're deciding what to do," answered Slocum. "You better keep the women inside. No use getting the braves riled up. Right now, they're moving slow and easy. Gunther may be right about the whiskey giving them a hangover."

But Madam Mamie, Trixie, and Debbie were already outside the building. They had come out to stand behind Slocum and stare at the Indians.

"Lord, they look so pretty," said Debbie. "They're the most beautiful men I've ever seen."

Slocum cleared his throat. "Now they'll be deciding whether to kill you or not."

"They look like great men," said Madam Mamie.

"They are," Slocum explained. "The Sioux believe they're kings of the world. You've given the war party a nice view of yourselves. Now you'd better get inside and stay there."

"But they're just men," protested Trixie. "They wouldn't hurt us."

"They could kill you without batting an eyelash," Slocum told her.

Trixie was stunned by Slocum's statement. She started to stammer in protest, then felt Madam Mamie's hand tighten over her wrist. "Come along, girls," said the older woman. "Best to follow John's advice. He knows about Indians."

Slocum stood alone outside of the stagecoach station. He watched the Indians across the river with a wary gaze. A half dozen of the braves leaped on their ponies, kicked the animals in the ribs, and raced across the meadow. They veered suddenly and splashed through the creek, yelping and laughing, their copper faces held high toward the heavens.

They stopped suddenly about forty feet from where Slocum stood. They dismounted by sliding back over the rumps of their animals. Laughing aloud, they held their feathered lances above their heads and looked at Slocum with their dark eyes. They were proud warriors: proud of their horsemanship, proud of their fighting ability, proud of the tough reputation they held among the other tribes.

Now the chief leaped up on his black and white pony and rode across the meadow. He crossed the creek and kicked his mount into a gallop as the animal moved swiftly past his warriors. The chief came thundering toward John Slocum, straight and tall in the saddle, ready to ride down the man from Georgia.

Slocum's fingers tightened on the Winchester as he stood before the charging pony. He suppressed the urge to shoot the chief, which would end the silly game of manhood. Unflinching, Slocum stood his ground and waited for the last moment to pull the trigger.

The chief kicked his pony in the ribs, smiled, and leaped off the animal. The pony went racing past Slocum, nostrils flared. The pony was so close that Slocum could have reached out and brushed against the charging beast.

Meanwhile, the chief landed on his feet a scant five

yards in front of Slocum. It seemed that an ordinary mortal would fall head over heels, but the chief retained his balance; he came to a halt, rocking back on his heels. He grinned. His expression was of great expectancy, as if John Slocum would applaud his performance.

Slocum heard a shuffle behind him, whirled, and saw that J. J. Findlay had come out of the building. The marshal leaned on his rude crutch and carried a Sharps repeating rifle in his free hand.

There was a fearful expression on the marshal's face. His eyes glittered with a feral gleam. Slocum noticed that Findlay's right cheek was twitching with a muscle tic.

"Figured you might need help," Findlay said. His voice was cracked and unnatural. "I see that Chief Fancy-pants is putting on a show for his braves."

Behind the chief, the painted braves began to yell and chant the glory of their leader. The Indians whooped, hollered, and broke into a ritualistic dance. They were paying homage to their chief, the greatest warrior of all time, a leader who could easily vanquish his enemies.

The Sioux chief plunged his feathered lance into the earth. He made a fist and pounded his copper chest. In the meadow, the braves roared their approval. Off to the side, an Indian brought out a drum and began to pound the head with his hands. The chief stepped toward Slocum without fear, stopping only when Slocum raised the Winchester a scant inch or two.

"He understands that," grinned Findlay.

The chief began to talk with a singsong beat. He pointed to the sky, calling out to the Great Spirit to look at these miserable pale-faced people. Such abominations should not be allowed to trespass on the land of the people, the Sioux. They should be driven off the land, back to the strange place from where they had come. They should be sent beyond the land that was sacred to the Dakota tribes. They were like white worms found under a rock in wet ground, said the chief.

The chief stepped back with a smug grin on his face. He folded his arms as his braves shouted their approval.

Slocum translated the chief's statement. "His name is Gray Wolf," Slocum explained. "He is the chief mucky-muck, the be-all of all times. He is the roughest, toughest Indian that ever lived, and his braves are meaner than deballed tomcats."

"What do they want?" asked Findlay.

"Booze," answered Slocum. "He knows Olson makes wine. He wants a few barrels of it. Right now, we're lucky because they've still got some of the whiskey they stole yesterday. So we don't have to make medicine with a bunch of hung-over Indians. That might be dangerous."

When the loud cheering of the Indians stopped, Slocum spoke to their chief. The Sioux were surprised at Slocum's mastery of their language. Slocum explained that his people were impressed that Gray Wolf and his braves had stopped at the stagecoach station. They were welcome to spend time with Slocum and his friends, who represented the Great White Father.

News about their visit was being sent to Washington, where the White Father lived, the great chief of many soldiers who carried sticks that killed from a distance. While the White Father was pleased with a visit from the Sioux, he had forbidden anyone to give whiskey to his guests.

"Besides, we do not have whiskey," Slocum said.

Gray Wolf spat. "There is whiskey in the barn. We have seen the kegs. My men have watched as the white man gathered the berries to brew the liquid that is like fire."

"That has been gone for two moons," Slocum said.

Gray Wolf spat again. "White man lies," he said.

Slocum ignored the insult. He repeated, "Whiskey is not available. Gray Wolf should take his warriors to Cheyenne to get whiskey."

As Slocum spoke, Gray Wolf shook back the black hair on his head. He raised his head and sneered with disdain. His braves let loose a loud, angry cry and looked on with puckered mouths and acid thoughts. Their black granite eyes glared with anger.

"We will take whiskey," said Gray Wolf in an angry voice.

Slocum watched the Sioux chieftain turn on his heel and walk away. "We will give you something to eat," said Slocum.

The Indian leader did not reply. He mounted his sturdy little pony and rode across the creek to where his warriors were gathered.

"Trouble is coming," said Findlay.

Slocum agreed. "We'd better get inside and get ready."

"You think they'll attack in daylight?" Findlay asked.

"Would you?"

"No."

"They'll probably wait until dark," said Slocum. "We'd better get ready and pray for a bright moon. They're spoiling for a fight. If I know the Sioux, they'll show off for each other most of the afternoon. Then they'll put on a war dance. They'll whoop and holler for a spell, building up their courage to attack tonight."

"Can we hold them off?" wondered Findlay.

"With luck," answered Slocum.

They remained inside the station house during the afternoon. The women were frightened because everyone knew a horrible story of what happened to female captives of the Indians. Madam Mamie told her girls to quit discussing such morbid subjects.

"I've heard that women are treated right nice by the Indians," the madam said, hoping to lighten the girls' spirits.

"Treated nice! That's a laugh," snorted Debbie. "I heard about this lady who was taken by the Bannocks or some such tribe. They took her to their camp, tied her up, and hauled her onto one of their lodgepoles. They dangled her up in the air and built a fire under her until the poor woman's feet and legs were roasted. She was still screaming when they cut her down and turned the dogs loose."

"They did that?" Trixie's voice was high-pitched and scared.

"That's what I was told by a drummer from Kansas City," said Debbie, crossing her heart.

"Hush up with such talk," snapped Madam Mamie.

"Yeah," agreed Bunny. "These menfolk ain't gonna let four prize pieces of pussy get taken by those redskins."

"That's right!" Dan Gunther grinned.

"It would be a crime," said Bunny.

Slocum laughed. "A waste of good talent."

"You reckon those Indians are coming after us?" wondered Debbie.

"Well, if they do we'd better be prepared," said Madam Mamie. She looked at Slocum, who was peering out a gun hole. "What are they doing out there?"

"Showing off," he replied. "Mostly running their ponies up and down the meadow, showing off their horsemanship."

"Fools!" said Debbie.

"They're good riders," said Slocum. "Probably the best horsemen in the world. A Sioux baby will be riding before it walks. They treasure their animals. A Sioux brave will go hungry to keep his pony fed. They're good."

Debbie asked, "You reckon we got a chance?"

"Sure," Slocum said. "They're armed with bows, arrows, and lances. Now, they're about the best around for accuracy with those weapons. But we got guns and plenty of ammunition. That gives us an edge. We're also holed up in here and they have to come in after us. All we have to do is make it expensive to get us."

"What does that mean?" asked Bunny.

"We kill a lot of them fast and quick," said Slocum.

"Which means we'd better teach you gals how to handle a rifle," added Findlay.

"Good idea," Slocum agreed.

Bunny shivered. "I'm scared of guns."

"I can't shoot anything," Debbie commented.

"You can load for us," said Slocum.

"Show them what to do," said Madam Mamie. "I don't intend to end up being roasted by some hostile tribe. And I don't want to be buried out in this godforsaken wilderness. The girls and I will do whatever is needed to be sure we get out of here."

"That's the spirit," said Dan Gunther. "Now, who's going to be in charge of this thing?"

"I nominate Slocum," said Findlay.

"I second it," said Gene Olson.

"We'll start with getting some grub rustled up," said Slocum. "I figure we have about three hours before sundown. We'll fight better on a full stomach."

"The condemned ate their last meal," said Debbie, crossing the room and heading toward the big iron stove.

"Hush your mouth," snapped the madam. "One more crack like that and I'll turn you over my knee."

"Yes, ma'am," answered Debbie.

9

The waning light of a dying sun crept over the meadow. The Sioux warriors waited until the sun dropped behind the western mountains. Then two warriors came back from the hills with wood for their bonfire. They gathered around as their chief, Gray Wolf, removed two flint rocks from his war pouch. He sparked the tinder to smoke, then flames, and added tiny bits of dried weeds until the kindling was ablaze.

When the fire was flaming like a beacon in the night, the Indians started their war dance. Their loud shouts and gyrations were accompanied by the boom of the war drum. Gray Wolf led the dancers as they moved around the fire. It was important for the warriors to have a dance prior to a raid. Warriors needed to steel themselves for battle. A dance was a time when a brave acted out his courage and strength, and sought the gift of safety from the Great Spirit. To most of the Indians, life was a game to be enjoyed. A brave was noted for his stylish class in the war dance, as well as his courage during battle.

Inside the stagecoach building, time passed with unnerving slowness. The women gathered around the table and played dominoes, occasionally arguing about the game. Slocum and Gene Olson maintained a lookout on the Indians through the gun holes. Slocum knew that some tribes used a war dance as part of their strategy during an attack. While some of the warriors danced, others sneaked up on their targeted enemies for a surprise attack.

J. J. Findlay sat sullenly in a chair in the front corner of the room, changing the bandage on his wounded leg. Findlay wanted one of the girls to help him, but no one had offered. So, with a glum expression on his face, he tore up a sheet and wrapped the fabric around his leg.

Findlay was a frightened man. His hands trembled, and, despite his strongest will, he was unable to stop his inner shuddering. He turned the chair away from the center of the room so the others wouldn't see his shaking hands.

The simple fact was that Findlay was afraid. He was a man who bluffed by nature, hiding his timidity behind a gruff facade. He had learned a thousand different ways of hiding his fear during the War Between the States. Once inducted, he had finagled his way out of the infantry and into an artillery unit. The men who manned the big cannons stayed well behind the lines, not up front where the man-to-man combat took place.

These old wartime tricks became useful when Findlay became a U.S. marshal appointed to the western territories. He had relied on hard men, like his two deputies buried back in Paradise Valley, to lead the way. He had learned in the Army that plenty of men were willing to follow orders. Some were too frightened to be labeled a coward. Others desperately wanted to be known as a hero. Still others were simpleminded and could easily be manipulated.

A hundred tricks were available to the man who didn't want to risk his life. He could hang back and allow another person to lead a charge. A single step backward would sometimes push the other fellow into the danger spot. Mainly, it was important to hang back and let the other fellow go in first.

Nevertheless, Findlay figured the odds were slim if the Sioux attacked. The Indians could surround the stagecoach station and hold out for a long siege. The building could be set blazing with fire arrows. Or the hay in the barn could be piled against the station and set afire. There were a million different ways to kill every white person in the building.

And what stuck in Findlay's craw, really stopped up his gullet, was the treasure map worth a fortune in gold. Deep down inside, deep down where he really lived, Findlay knew there was gold in the cave. He didn't believe in second sight, or any form of foreknowledge, but he knew instinctively that the map was true.

Now fate was about to deal Findlay a bad hand of cards from the bottom of the deck. He would be dead before his riches could be enjoyed. It wasn't fair that a man had a treasure map, a bum leg, and was encircled by a band of whooping Indians. He wished somehow that the clock could be turned back, that events had not put him in this dangerous position.

When the new bandage was applied to his leg, Findlay picked up his crutch and limped over to the fireplace. He tossed the old, bloody bandages into the fireplace, where a smoldering fire was burning beneath a cast-iron pot of pinto beans.

He leaned on his crutch and looked around the room. Slocum was on a ladder on the back wall oiling the hinges of a door opening to the roof. Gene Olson had pulled a wooden box from beneath the bed and was checking the contents, whatever they were. Dan Gunther and the women were gathered around the table, the dominoes laid aside and a deck of cards brought out.

Findlay limped to the center of the room. "I have an announcement to make," said the marshal. "An important notice to everyone in this room."

Everyone looked in the marshal's direction. Slocum crawled down the ladder and looked at Findlay with a puzzled expression. He wondered if the marshal's craziness was returning.

"This is not something I thought I'd ever do," said Findlay.

"Well, get to it," said Gunther.

Findlay balanced himself on his crutch and slipped his left hand into his pocket. "I don't know if any of us will be alive tomorrow morning. Some or all of us may be killed. I have a map here"—and he held up the large piece of sheepskin—"that shows where a lot of gold can be found. If I don't make it through until morning, this map belongs to whoever wants to go after the gold."

A flurry of questions followed Findlay's announcement. He answered each query with the information he possessed about the map. The women were excited by the prospect of finding gold, but the men had questions about the map.

"Hell, this doesn't say where the cave is located," said Gene Olson. "It could be anywhere."

"I was told it was somewhere in the Black Hills," said Findlay.

"Buddy, that's a fairly large piece of territory," Olson responded.

"And sacred land for the Sioux," added Dan Gunther. "Let me look at that thing."

Findlay spread the map out on the table. He picked up a skinning knife and pointed to the cave shaped like an eye. "The treasure is supposed to be in there," the marshal said. "We can–"

Slocum interrupted. "The map is dandy," he said. "But we'd better get back to the job at hand. It's getting dark out, and, if you listen, you'll discover the Sioux have stopped drumming. They should be preparing to attack."

"I'm ready for them," said Gunther, picking up a Sharps repeating rifle.

Slocum nodded, then glanced in Findlay's direction. "You cover one of the gun holes. Olson, you want to take a little walk?"

"Now?" The Swede looked confused.

"We'll mosey outside and scout around," said Slocum. "We might run into a few visitors."

"Should I bring my rifle?"

"Leave it," advised Slocum. "A knife and pistol are all you're going to need. If we run into Indians we'll be fighting man-to-man. Whoever is at the gun holes be sure you're not firing at us."

"Be careful," whispered Madam Mamie.

"We're just scouting out the territory," said Slocum. "I'll knock twice on the door before coming in."

He checked his pistols, then made sure the big-bladed knife holstered on his hip was easy to draw. Next, he pulled off his boots and indicated that Gene

Olson should also remove his brogan shoes.

Dan Gunther shielded the light of the oil lamp to prevent silhouettes showing through the open door. Slocum and Gene Olson were barefooted as they slipped out. The Swede followed Slocum to the middle of the yard, his tender feet crunching on the sharp gravel. They halted there and waited for their eyes to adjust to the darkness.

Olson nudged Slocum as they saw a shadowy figure coming from the direction of the creek. Slocum had figured the Sioux would send out scouts to test the defenses of the whites.

Slocum pulled his knife and crept toward the oncoming shadow. Then, through the dimness, Slocum lost sight of the Indian. He remained stationary and waited for some sign of the enemy. A moment passed before he saw a vague movement at ground level. The brave was crawling forward on all fours.

Slocum waited until the Indian was within striking distance. Then he leaped forward with his knife held firmly in his hand. Slocum's body slammed down hard against the Indian's back. The brave let loose with a small grunting sound. The Indian had started to scream, but his cry was cut off when Slocum's thumb pressed against the brave's Adam's apple.

The Indian twisted beneath Slocum, who plunged the blade deep into the man's side. Once, twice, three times the knife rose and slashed into the Indian's body. Then the Indian went slack. To make certain the Indian was dead, Slocum slid the sharp edge of the blade deep and harshly across the man's throat.

Slocum's senses were sharp, acute to the smallest sound. Off to his left he heard a muffled scuffling noise. He moved in that direction and found Gene Olson with his hand clamped over a brave's mouth. The Indian was struggling to get away from the giant Swede.

"It's me," whispered Slocum, moving up to Olson's side.

The Swede slammed his knife into the Indian's shoulder, withdrew it, and plunged the blade into the brave's chest.

Quickly, Slocum lashed out with his blade and cut the Indian's throat.

"Thanks," whispered Olson. He started to stand up but was knocked back by a swinging blow from an Indian lance.

Slocum saw dark shadows running toward him through the creek. He drew his revolver and quickly fired at point-blank range. The braves retreated back across the creek.

Slocum helped Olson to his feet. "You hurt?"

"Just groggy."

"Let's get back inside," Slocum said.

Olson agreed. "Hand-to-hand war ain't my cup of tea."

Quickly they made their way to the front of the building. Slocum rapped lightly on the door, which was opened by Dan Gunther.

"This is war," Olson declared. "I didn't think they would attack. Now they've got me riled up. Those Sioux have been pretty good boys, for the most part. Now they're going to take a licking."

Slocum grinned. "Glad to hear it."

"Any objections to dynamite?"

Slocum was surprised. "You got some?"

"A whole box over there."

"What's your plan?"

"Sneak up on the roof and send a couple sticks in

their direction." Olson went over and pulled a box from a pile of clutter in the corner of the room.

Findlay came over. "Jesus, you keep that stuff in here? I've been told dynamite is dangerous."

Gene Olson pulled a half-dozen sticks of dynamite from the box. "Depends on how you handle it," he said. "The stuff is pretty stable unless she gets to sweating. Then the stuff gets a little dicey. And it ain't much of a problem unless you get careless."

"I'm not risking my life," said the marshal. He turned and walked away.

"Dynamite ain't like black powder," Olson told Slocum. "Powder will blow if you think bad about it. Dynamite does exactly what you tell it to do."

"I don't know much about it," Slocum admitted.

"One of my Swedish countrymen invented it," Olson said, cutting fuses. "His name was Nobel. A contrary cuss because he kept trying to get it right. Blowed up most of his family and half the town before he discovered the right mixture."

"Why do you have dynamite out here?" Slocum wondered.

"Company sent it out. I been planning to check out what looks like a coal seam on the other side of the valley. Dynamite works fastern'n shoveling for mining."

As he talked, Olson fixed detonators and short fuses to the dynamite sticks.

"We'll need something to light them with," said Slocum. "Anyone got a cheroot?"

Dan Gunther raced across the room and pulled a leather cheroot holder from the pocket of his jacket. He pulled three of the long, dark cigars from the case. "Want me to light them?" he asked.

"Here, I'll help," said Trixie. She took one of the cheroots and went over to the fireplace. A moment later she was holding an ember on a long stick up to the stogie.

Suddenly, the furious sound of the war party came from outside. Something heavy thudded against the door.

"They're trying to ram it down," cried Findlay.

Madam Mamie was peering through a gun hole. "They're lighting arrows."

"They'll shoot them onto the roof," said Slocum.

Outside, the Indians howled and roared as their ponies carried the warriors around the building.

An arrow slammed deep into the wood near a gun hole. Debbie Winters, who had been watching through the opening, pulled back with a look of dismay on her face.

"Can you see good enough to shoot?" Slocum yelled.

"Too dark," said Madam Mamie.

"Squeeze off a couple shots," he yelled. "Let 'em know we're here."

The boom of Madam Mamie's carbine drowned out the other noise.

Slocum looked down at Gene Olson, who was fixing another dozen sticks of dynamite.

"This stuff ready?" Slocum asked, picking up a handful of sticks.

"Light it and throw fast," grunted Olson. "Don't wait around or you'll get blowed to kingdom come."

Slocum took a strong drag on his cheroot. "I'll be up on the roof," he said.

"Don't worry," Olson said, priming more dynamite. "We'll hear you."

Slocum stuffed his pockets with dynamite sticks and

hurried up the ladder on the far wall of the room. He looked back as he came up to the trapdoor opening onto the roof. J. J. Findlay was sitting in a rocking chair, his shotgun aimed toward the door. The power of the battering log could be seen as the hinges of the door twisted—but held—under the blows.

Then the trapdoor was open and Slocum raised his head into the open air. A flaming arrow had been shot into the side of the building. Down below, the thunderous hooves of Indian ponies sounded in the darkness. A cacophony of yells, shouts, and roars accompanied the Indians as they circled the stagecoach station.

Slocum balanced himself on the ladder, leaning against the side of the trapdoor frame. He pulled a stick of dynamite from his pocket and held the cheroot against the fuse. The short piece of string sparked to life as Slocum tossed the stick over the roof toward the front door of the building.

He was lighting another stick of dynamite when the first stick exploded. The terrible roar boomed through the night. The darkness was rent by a split-second blast of powerful white-orange light.

The next stick was tossed to the side of the building. That blast was accompanied by the scream of a dying Indian and the sound of a pony screaming in the dark.

In less than a minute Slocum hurled all the sticks of dynamite at the attacking Indians. He heard the cries of dying warriors, the whimper of wounded animals. Vaguely, his stomach shifted and he felt nauseous.

Then, above the noisy din, came the sound of a Sioux drum beating out a message of retreat. A moment was required for the Indians to receive the message, then they turned their ponies away from the building.

Slocum could hear the hoofbeats as the Indians rode away.

After waiting several minutes, Slocum and Gene Olson lit a coal-oil lantern and went outside to inspect the carnage. The damage was surprisingly light considering the power of the dynamite. Two Indian ponies were down on the ground and dying. Slocum held the light while Gene Olson shot the animals with a carbine.

They found two braves off to the side of the front door. Both of the Indians were dead. Next, they made a wary tour of the front yard, looking under the two covered wagons for signs of wounded men. Then they started around the side of the building.

They had gone around two sides of the building when a light moaning noise came from the direction of the barn. The two men moved with caution until they discovered a lone Indian brave. He was lying in a patch of weeds near the barn, wearing deerskin leggings and a fringed, beaded shirt. An eagle's feather was tucked in a leather band worn around his head. The Indian's scalp was cut. Blood flowed through his black hair and down onto his copper cheeks.

Gene Olson held up the lantern. "Do we kill him or leave him be?" he asked.

Slocum handed his pistol to the Swede. "I'll check him out. Shoot if he gets disagreeable."

Bending over, Slocum saw that the cut in the Indian's scalp was not deep.

"He alive?" asked Olson.

"Yeah."

"Want some help to drag him inside?"

Slocum stood up. He was thoughtful for a moment.

"Yeah, run in and get Dan Gunther. Let's save the poor devil if we can."

Slocum took the lantern and stood quietly while Olson went inside the house. A couple of minutes went by, then Olson reappeared with Gunther. Together, the two men carried the limp body into the stagecoach building.

They started to lay the Indian on the cornshuck mattress. But Madam Mamie complained that his blood would stain the mattress cover. Instead, they spread an old blanket on the floor and laid the Indian in front of the fireplace.

"What's he doing in here?" demanded Madam Mamie.

"He's hurt," said Slocum.

"You're helping him after he tried to kill us?" This came from Debbie Winters.

"He's a human being," snapped Gene Olson.

"Well, I never..." muttered Trixie. "Stand here and jabber while the poor thing bleeds to death. I'm going to see if we can fix him up."

"Just be careful," cautioned Slocum. "He's knocked out."

"Unconscious or not," said Trixie, "I'll do what I can for him."

"Don't bother yourself," snarled Findlay. "Why don't we throw him outside with the other trash?"

Slocum walked over to the washstand and filled a basin with water. He picked up a washcloth and walked back to where the Indian was stretched out.

"Here," said Trixie, taking the basin of water. "Let me wash him up." She placed a damp cloth on the side of the Indian's scalp.

Suddenly, the unconscious figure stiffened and

moaned loudly. The Indian leaped up, his dark eyes blazing with anger.

He looked around wildly, then his gaze focused on a knife lying beside the map on the table.

The Indian made a lunge for the blade.

10

Later, the story would be told over a thousand campfires in the West. Some yarn-spinners would claim the whole thing smacked of a miracle, something dreamed up by angelic beings in Heaven. Others would declare the whole kit and caboodle was the figment of someone's overactive imagination. Still others would just recite the facts and let their listeners judge for themselves.

When the Sioux brave made a lunge for the knife on the table, John Slocum's hand shot out and his fingers clasped the warrior's wrist. The Indian twisted around and his right knee hammered a deflecting blow up into Slocum's groin. Slocum bent forward, but he did not let loose of the Indian's arm. He shoved his shoulder into the warrior's midsection, pushing him back. The Indian went sprawling onto the floor. He tried to get up, but Slocum connected with a hard right cross against the side of the brave's forehead.

The Indian passed out again.

"Of all the dumb deals," cried J. J. Findlay, limping

114

across the room on his makeshift crutch, his revolver held in his free hand. "You carry that Indian in here and let him almost murder one of us. I'm killing that red devil right now. Here, Olson! You and Gunther help me carry him outside."

Slocum stood up. He took a deep breath to ease the pain in his groin. He motioned for Olson and Gunther to relax. "Easy does it," he told the marshal. "It was my mistake not to tie him up."

Findlay leaned on his crutch and snapped the toe of his boot against the Indian's shoulder. "A good Indian is a dead one," he said viciously.

"I've hunted with the Sioux," Slocum said. "They're good people."

"They're savages!" cried Findlay in a shrill voice. He leaned against the table and started to raise his crutch to strike the Indian.

"Don't hit him," Slocum said. "You answer to me if you do."

Findlay looked into Slocum's steel-hard face. The man from Georgia's gaze was hard and unforgiving.

"Well, he's just a redskin." Findlay shook his head from side to side, as if in wonderment at Slocum's unusual behavior.

"Somebody get me a dipper of water," Slocum said.

Bunny was closest to the washstand. She dipped the tin dipper into the bucket of drinking water and handed it to Slocum.

"Did he hurt you down there?" Bunny asked. "I'd hate to think you was banged up real bad."

"He didn't hit the target," Slocum said, taking the dipper from the girl.

"That's real good news," Bunny said, smiling.

"Maybe . . . if you want to, that is . . . we can go for a walk later."

"Let me wake this fellow up first." Slocum poured the dipper of cold water on the face of the unconscious Sioux.

The Indian made a sputtering sound, licked his lips, and opened his eyes.

Slocum looked down and spoke in the Sioux language. "Don't try anything. We don't want to kill you."

The Indian slowly rose to a sitting position. He looked around with an apprehensive expression. He shook his head, once, twice, and knuckled his eyes. "Where am I?" he asked in distinctly pronounced English.

Everyone gathered around the Indian, because a brave with a good command of the English language was unusual. He reached up and adjusted the two long braids of black hair that hung down on each side of his face.

"Stagecoach station," Slocum replied.

"This isn't the land of the Great Spirit?" The hint of a smile tugged at the edges of the Indian's lips.

"I'm afraid not." Slocum let his palm rest on the butt of his revolver. "We don't want to hurt you. Will you give me your promise not to do anything foolish?"

"Hell, man, I'm outgunned," said the Sioux.

"What's your name?"

"The Indians call me He-Who-Walks-Like-Thunder," answered the Indian. "The folks in St. Louis called me Big Thunder."

"St. Louis?" Madam Mamie raised her eyebrows.

"Yes, ma'am," answered Big Thunder.

"How in the world did you get there?" Bunny wanted to know.

"A couple of trappers spent several winters in my village," Big Thunder explained. "One trapper taught me to speak your tongue. He promised to take me to St. Louis if I'd lead him to a big valley of beaver. We spent a winter trapping and went down to St. Louis."

"Land's sake," said Debbie Winters. "You've led an interesting life."

"What were you doing with this war party?" Gene Olson wanted to know.

"Trying to prove I'm a man."

"How so?"

"I got tired of living in St. Louis and figured the time had come to go back to my people," Big Thunder explained. "I didn't fit in the city too well. But I learned that I'm too much of a white man to be an Indian."

Olson said, "That doesn't answer why you were on the warpath."

"The braves kept bragging about how they were better than me," Big Thunder explained. "They kept taunting me until I agreed to go on the warpath with them. It was either that or get shoved off with the women."

Bunny protested, "But you were trying to kill us."

"Nope. I was just riding around outside yelling and hollering when something made a big noise. Then I woke up in here." Big Thunder looked up into Slocum's face. "Can I get up?"

"Just behave yourself," Slocum answered.

The Indian stood up. He was unsteady on his feet and laid his hand on the edge of the table for support. His gaze took in the branded outline of the sheepskin map.

"Someone's been up in my part of the country," said Big Thunder. "That map is pretty good. I know that country. That's—"

It was as far as Big Thunder got. Instantly, the atmosphere in the stagecoach station was electrified with tension. J. J. Findlay started to run toward the table, forgot to use his crutch, pressed down on his bad leg, and lurched against a chair. Gritting his teeth, the marshal maintained his balance and hobbled over to stand beside Big Thunder.

Madam Mamie and her girls pressed in toward the Indian. Gene Olson and Dan Gunther circled the table and came up behind the brave. John Slocum reached out and picked up the knife lying on the table.

Big Thunder looked around with an astonished expression. "What did I do?" he inquired.

Findlay said, "You said you knew the country on the map."

"Sure."

"You could take us there?"

"I guess so," replied the Indian.

"There's gold there!" cried Bunny. "We're going to be rich!"

"Lordy!" shouted Debbie. "We can have anything we want!"

J. J. Findlay leaned against the table. His hand snaked out and grabbed the map. "I'd better keep this in a safe place," the marshal said. He glanced over at Big Thunder. "What would we need to get to the land on the map?"

Big Thunder shrugged. "Horses and some food. Or, if need be, we can walk, but the trip would take a while. And my people don't like outsiders messing around in there."

Findlay's eyes gleamed with excitement. "But you could get us to this place?"

"Sure. No problem," said the Indian.

"When can we start?"

"You're forgetting the most important part," said Big Thunder.

"Which is?" snapped Findlay.

"What do I get out of it?" asked Big Thunder.

"Half of the gold," Findlay said.

Slocum spoke up. "You're dang poor on totaling things up, Findlay. Half for me. Another half for the Indian. Your share won't amount to very much. It'll be mighty slim."

"You're not needed now, Slocum," said the marshal. "Your share depended on you finding the cave."

Slocum chuckled. "I know. You'll call when you need something."

Findlay hobbled over and sat down in a battered oak chair. "You know what I mean, Slocum. Business is . . . well, business. A man has to look out for himself. I got to take care of number one."

Slocum nodded. "I should have thought like that back in Paradise Valley."

"You'll get paid! Don't worry about it!" A harsh undertone edged the marshal's voice.

Slocum turned his back on the marshal. He walked over and took Bunny's hand. "You still want to go for that walk?"

The girl looked up with a pleased expression. "I'd love it, kind sir."

The moon had come out, a silver orb hanging in a black velvet sky. They walked through the moon-blanched valley and stopped in a small grove of cottonwood trees beside the stream. The silvery moonlight enhanced Bunny's beauty as she looked up into Slocum's eyes.

"A penny for your thoughts, sir," she whispered.

"I was thinking how beautiful you are."

"Mrs. Brawshaw would be pleased."

"Who's she?"

"My mother."

"Bless her," he said. "She turns out a perfect product."

Bunny smiled contentedly. "You really think so?"

"I sure do." Slocum looked down into the cameo perfection of her face. Her features held a wholesome appeal that could win a man's heart. She was young enough to make a man want to take her in his arms, to protect her forever from violence, deception, and the dreadful realities of life.

"How old are you, Bunny?"

"Twenty-two."

"How long have you been with Madam Mamie?"

"Less than a year."

"Do you like being a working girl?"

She sighed. "I'd like to find a fellow of my own and settle down."

"What's stopping you?"

She shrugged. "I haven't found the right man."

"You been looking?"

She giggled. "Slocum, you may be experienced . . . but you don't know women and their wiles. Every woman is looking for a man when she's single. That's part of our feminine nature."

"No fellow fits your requirements?"

"A couple did," the girl replied. "But for one reason or another it didn't work out. I don't have any education, and my looks and a love of cock is all I got going for me. It stands to reason I'd end up as a working girl. *You* would do right nice, but you move around too much. I want a man who likes being settled down."

"How did you know I roam around?"

The tip of her pink tongue darted out and licked her lips. "I asked Findlay about you. Just checking to see what kind of person you were."

"What did he say?"

"That you've been roaming the West for a long time . . . since the war."

"He's right," Slocum said.

"I don't like Findlay. He's dangerous."

"Findlay? He's off in his head because of his bad leg."

"He's nasty."

"Naw. Just getting used to limping for the rest of his life."

"Just watch out for him," Bunny said. Suddenly she raised up on her tiptoes and placed her warm lips against his. Her tongue was a fiery arrow that darted into his mouth.

Her hands grasped the growing firmness of his manhood, and her fingers made a slow, circular motion. Then she undid the buttons of his pants and her palm encircled his throbbing flesh. Slocum stiffened instantly as she stroked him with a hard, tight movement.

She drew back from his lips. "I do like to pleasure a man with my mouth," she said.

Then she dropped to her knees and knelt before him. Her full lips parted, and her pink tongue came out to moisten them. Slocum stroked the golden curls on her thrusting head. Her tongue made a fluttering butterfly movement against his cock. Then he throbbed with desire as her mouth and lips engulfed him. With a tiny moan of pleasure, she drew him inside her hot, moist mouth.

Slocum felt the warm sensation as her lips, tongue, and mouth moved over him like a flaming wave . . .

When it was over, Bunny buttoned his trousers and stood up. "There," she said, hugging him for a moment. "I've been wanting to give you that since I first saw you."

Slocum smiled. "I think sleep will come easy tonight."

"If it doesn't," Bunny smiled, "let me know and we'll try a return engagement. I aim to please, sir."

"Do we need a rehearsal?" asked Slocum.

"No sir, just a nice, hard cock."

"You make me want to settle down."

"You're a good man, Slocum, but not for me."

Slocum was surprised by her reaction. "I don't understand what's wrong with me," he said with mock anger.

"You're a rolling stone. And, baby, those fast-moving rocks are interesting, but they don't gather up many greenbacks. This little girl wants a husband with lots of cash. Sweetness and love always goes away. Nothing lasts forever, and change is the only thing in life that's permanent. I want lots of greenback dollars to keep me warm on a cold winter night."

Slocum laughed. "You think money is that important?"

"Don't you?"

"I never had it."

"How do you know it wouldn't ease your way through life?" she asked.

"Well, I'm a lucky person. Money would just tie me down. I got an easy row to hoe in life. I pretty much do what I want to."

"Most people don't have that choice. They're drones. Or drudges."

"That's their own fault."

"No, it ain't," Bunny said. "Most folks get trapped. They get stuck in a rut. They're not able to get out because maybe they don't have the money, the education, or the know-how to make their way in the world. I've been working with Madam Mamie for almost a year. Down in Dodge City, I saw those cowboys coming up with the cattle herds from Texas. Some of those poor fellows had never seen a pretty girl until they hit Dodge. Poor babies. They wouldn't last ten minutes in a fast town like Chicago, or Rock Island, Illinois."

They left the grove of trees and turned back toward the stagecoach station. Slocum wished he could spend the night out under the stars with this warm-blooded young woman. But that wouldn't be a responsible choice, because, he knew, everyone was tense after the Indian attack. Guards would have to be posted during the night, just in case the war party came back. He would have to sleep light, keep an eye on Big Thunder, and keep the others from fighting over Findlay's so-called treasure map. Things were becoming hectic.

The sound of an argument drifted out of the stagecoach station as Slocum and Bunny walked into the yard. Slocum could hear Gene Olson yelling in a loud voice. Madam Mamie was shrieking like a female polecat undergoing a breach birth.

"Stay behind me," Slocum told Bunny. "I'll go in first."

Slocum kicked open the door.

J. J. Findlay spun around, balancing himself on his crutch. The marshal had a six-gun in his hand. Big Thunder stood off to the side of the room, while the others were crowded in the back.

"Stop him!" shrieked Madam Mamie.

"He's gone crazy!" wailed Debbie.

"He's taking the map!" cried Trixie.

Slocum reached out and grabbed the gun from Findlay's hand. "What's going on?" he demanded.

"These fools want my gold," Findlay said lamely. "I'm not sharing anything with a bunch of doxies. I was planning on leaving."

"Leave, my foot!" complained Madam Mamie. "He was going to kidnap that poor Indian."

Findlay smiled weakly. "Well, hell, Slocum. The Indian knows where the cave is."

Slocum looked at Big Thunder. "You going with him?"

"Damn little choice!" said the Indian. "He has a gun."

Madam Mamie walked over and stood before J. J. Findlay, wagging her finger at the marshal. "You greedy creature! We need that gold as much as you do. These girls have had a hard life. They've rubbed their bodies up against some of the sourest-smelling galoots in Dodge City. They've had to screw men who were so ugly their mothers should have drowned them."

Findlay glanced over at Gene Olson. "Get out your fiddle, Swede. We need some sad music to go along with this whore's lament."

"Now the whole lot of us are stony broke. Wintering in Dodge City was a mistake," Madam Mamie went on. "We're busted. We ain't got two beans to rub together for a bowl of soup. Getting part of that treasure would fix us up in grand style."

"Well, you're not going to get it," said Findlay with a determined expression. "The gold belongs to me."

Madam Mamie put her hands on her hips. She

looked at Slocum with a fiery glint in her eyes. "What do you say, Slocum?" she demanded.

Slocum shook his head wearily. "The treasure map belongs to Findlay," he said. "If he wants to head out in the morning, I'm ready to hit the trail with him. What do you say, J. J.?"

"Let's ride," answered the marshal.

"I'll go along," chimed in Big Thunder.

"And leave us here?" wailed Madam Mamie.

"Gunther has that wagonload of guns to deliver in Deadwood. We'll ride along with you folks to Deadwood. Then we split up. You women were heading for Deadwood when you came in here. You can make a fortune in a boomtown."

"Of all the thievin' nerve," snapped Madam Mamie. She spun around on the heels of her patent leather shoes, went over, and flung herself down on the cornshuck bed.

"You got nerve," said Bunny. "After all I done for you tonight. Madam Mamie's had a hard life."

"That don't give her call to cut in on Findlay's deal," Slocum told the girl.

11

A week after leaving the stagecoach station, Slocum led
his group into Deadwood. It was a typical frontier
boomtown, named after the burnt timber on one side of
the gulch. The town consisted of tents, clapboard
houses and business establishments, a few livery
stables, and scores of gambling halls, saloons, and
houses of ill repute.

The town was crowded with gold seekers who hoped
to get rich quick. They hurried out into the mountains
with picks, shovels, and placer pans to grab their share
of the riches. They dug shafts into the earth, right down
to bedrock, shoveling and clawing for the precious yellow metal. They found gold in the cracks and crevices
of the mountains, gold that had been resting there since
the mountain chain was formed.

They also washed the gold from the streams, sacked
it, hid it from their friends and partners, and prayed to
the Creator for a shot at the mother lode. They carried
the prized metal into town, watched the assay man

weigh it, and laughed as he counted out the greenback dollars and gold coins for payment.

Gold kept them going like men seized by fever. Gold could turn a stumblebum into an instant millionaire, make an old man feel young, a young fool sound wise; and the metal paid for whiskey, women, and good times with people who wanted to be your friend.

Every man went out into the wilderness with hopes of becoming wealthy. They came back in a few days, rich or poor, elated with their luck, or hangdog hungover with poor pickings. Regardless of their fortune, they ate, slept, and spent most of their hours in saloons swilling down rotgut whiskey.

They told the other drinkers about their big deals, lied about their accomplishments, and pushed, shoved, bought, sold, robbed, and bartered their neighbors for another chance at riches. A man could get his throat cut for a half ounce of gold in Deadwood, find old friends from other boomtowns, or fall down drunk in a ditch and come up holding a half-pound gold nugget.

John Slocum was happy to be in Deadwood. The trip to the booming town had not been the happiest of journeys. Madam Mamie and her flock of soiled doves were angry about not getting a share of Findlay's gold. The women had been waspish, sharp-tongued, and given to venomous remarks.

J. J. Findlay had improved his outlook on life. The U.S. marshal was given to talking about what he planned on doing with his sudden wealth. At first, that talk had irritated Slocum because he knew gold hunting was a risky enterprise. Then Slocum decided that even a lawman needed to dream once in a while.

Big Thunder had proven that an Indian could have a sense of humor. He carried his share of trail duty, laughed, and regaled the women with outrageous stories about his bravery. The women doted on the Indian, and, while Slocum and Findlay slept alone, Big Thunder was always going off in the brush with one of the girls.

"Hell, red skin is popular," Big Thunder laughed one evening after a stroll into the brush with Debbie Winters. "The girls have orders from Madam Mamie to cut off you gents. Somebody has to do the dirty work, so I'm taking up the slack."

Dan Gunther was also doing well in the woman department. The teamster had seemingly forgotten his wife back in Cheyenne; at least his rigid attitude toward his marriage vows had loosened. Gunther and Trixie were bedding down together each night, holding hands during the day, and acting like two moonstruck youngsters. Gunther had tried to explain his actions to Slocum, who replied that every man did what he had to do.

Now, leading the wagons and pack animals into Deadwood, Slocum was glad to be in town. The laughing, talking, yelling crowd of people on the street indicated that Deadwood was a lively place. Slocum intended to stay over in Deadwood for a couple of days, buy the gear for the trip into the mountains, and spend some time in a saloon with a few cold beers.

Slocum led his group to a livery stable on the edge of town. Madam Mamie sniffed a quick thanks, then parked her wagon and called for her girls to gather round.

"I'll see you later," Trixie told Dan Gunther, tenderly kissing the teamster's chin.

"God, honey, I love you," said Gunther.

"Do something about it," said Trixie, walking away with the other women.

"Like what?" Gunther called after her.

"You know what," she yelled back.

Gunther looked like a loveless calf. "God, she's the love of my life."

"More like lust," chuckled Slocum. "Love 'em and leave 'em is the right motto. Else you end up with twenty wives sitting around and screeching at each other."

"Maybe you're right," the teamster agreed. "Well, time for me to get to a saloon and drown my sorrows. Where are you guys staying?"

"We're camping out here by the livery stable," Slocum said. "I figure the chances of getting a hotel room are pretty slim."

"Besides," added Findlay, "it'll save money."

"Slocum, Findlay, and Big Thunder watched the teamster walk away.

"He'll be pickled in another two hours," said Findlay.

"He needs it," the Indian declared. "That Trixie is a sweet little lay."

Slocum looked sharply at the Indian. "How do you know that?"

Big Thunder grinned. "Guessing, Slocum, just guessing. I don't poach another man's punchboard."

"You gents can stand and chat," Slocum said. "I'm going to wash the dust from my gullet with a few beers. I'll meet you back here tonight."

"What about me?" asked Big Thunder. "Is it safe for me to walk around the streets?"

"Hell, I don't know," admitted Slocum. "Stick close to Findlay. He's a U.S. marshal. He can protect you."

"Come along, red man," grinned Findlay. "I want to find someone to check out this leg of mine."

"How is it doing?" Slocum asked.

"A helluva lot better than I thought," Findlay replied. "A couple days of rest and I may be able to throw away my crutch."

Slocum walked to the Dakota Lady Saloon and Dance Hall. The establishment was the largest drinking place in Deadwood. It consisted of a large room, loud and noisy, with a chorus line of dancing girls jiggling to a band consisting of a fiddler, piano, and banjo player. Slocum elbowed through the crowd, gave his order to the harried bartender, and paid for his beer.

He sipped the cold brew and glanced toward the stage. Several girls were onstage flaunting their legs and breasts in a seemingly unrehearsed version of hurdy-gurdy dancing. The women were fairly attractive, the music was loud, and the yelling, cursing crowd of men were pleased with the performance.

After finishing his first glass, Slocum ordered another beer and wandered over to the gambling section of the saloon. He was quick to note that the wheels were rigged and the cards were marked or shaved.

Dan Gunther was standing by a roulette wheel, playing against the rigged equipment. Slocum watched the teamster lose several bets in a row. Then the man from Georgia wandered over and tapped Gunther's shoulder. "Want a beer?" Slocum asked.

Gunther smiled. "Sure. Anything beats giving my money away."

They wormed their way across the room, and Slocum bought a couple of beers. Gunther lamented his loss of Trixie's attentions and said he would never get over the loss of the girl's affections.

"I'll pay for a tumble at a brothel," said Slocum.

Gunther swilled down the remainder of his beer.

"Hell, I can't pass up an opportunity like that."

Slocum grinned. "Man, you're overwhelmed with grief."

"Get it while she's hot, especially if you're paying," chuckled Gunther.

They left the saloon and walked to a large stone building on the outskirts of town with a red lamp in the window. A passerby informed them that the building housed Boris Hunter's Brothel. The door was opened by a large, bald-headed man with thick arms and a powerful build. The two men were led into a parlor, where they took a seat on a horsehair sofa.

The big man, who said his name was Boris, clapped his hands. Four women in skimpy attire came sashaying into the parlor. As the women paraded around the room, Boris encouraged the men to select their favorite.

"They're all good in bed," said Boris, in a singsong manner. "One dollar is all you need, gents, to make your selection! Time is money, sirs, for these girls. Don't take too long, because the women get anxious about who you will pick. You won't find any virgins, gentlemen, but you will be satisfied. The girls do it French. They do it Greek. They do it in the missionary position. They will do it however you want it—provided you can explain the directions. If you got something really, really kinky that involves things people don't talk about . . . well, you check with me first. The law of the land is that kinky always costs extra!"

Gunther hesitated in making his choice. All of the women looked appealing. At last, under the urging of Boris's singsong patter, the teamster picked a petite girl with an hourglass figure. She had large, heavy breasts, a small waist, and attractive legs. Her brown hair was cut short in an attractive style.

The girl took Gunther's hand and led him out of the parlor into a bedroom. "My name is Anita," she said. "What's yours?"

Gunther introduced himself. He sat down on the edge of the bed, removed his boots, and pulled off his pants. "I'm ready," he said, lying back on the bed.

"Not so fast," Anita said. "I got to milk you first."

Gunther looked puzzled.

"Stand up, honey."

Gunther complied.

"Come over here," Anita said.

"What's going on?" asked Gunther.

"We have to test you," Anita explained. "Boris makes us check all of our customers."

She pulled Gunther closer to a washstand as she picked up a towel. Her fingers tightened around his flesh. She made several drawing motions.

"Like milking a cow," husked Gunther. He put his arm around the girl's shoulder. He was aroused with her closeness, the scent of her perfume.

"Holy saints!" Anita loosened her grip on his throbbing member.

She tossed the towel on the washstand.

She pushed Gunther back against the wall.

"You bastard!" The girl's voice was sharp, vicious in tone. "The nerve you've got, you diseased pervert. You come walking in here with a bad pecker!"

"What? Whatta you mean?" Gunther frowned.

The girl swept past Dan Gunther, opened the door, and yelled down the hall, "Boris! Hey, Boris!" Her scream was loud and shrill. "I got a bad case of clap in here!"

"What are you screaming about?" demanded Gunther.

The woman backed away. "Keep your distance! I milked your pecker and pus come out. You got the clap!"

"What's that?" Gunther was stunned.

"Your pecker is tainted, big boy. You're not screwing me or anyone else in this house."

Dan Gunther couldn't believe what the woman was saying.

"The pox, mister! You got a bad case of love sickness!" screamed Anita. "What kind of person are you? Come waltzing in here with a dose of the clap and expecting service. You got some nerve!" With a flouncing motion of her smooth, white shoulders, Anita started down the hall.

Gunther grabbed her arm and pulled her back to him. "You're mistaken, honey! I'm a married man!"

Anita tried to pull away. She yelled. "Boris, where are you?"

"Don't scream!" pleaded Gunther. "You'll get everyone upset."

"Look here!" The girl twisted out of his grasp, went into the room, and picked the towel up off the washbasin. "See that ugly pus there? Well, mister, that come out of your pecker! You've been with some dirty hussy! She infected your pecker! Boris was right! Oh lord, was he ever right! Always milk the damned things, else you'll end up with a bad dose."

Gunther stared at the mess on the towel with a disbelieving expression. "Ah, no way," he said. "That didn't come out of me. I'm married."

"Then, baby, your wife has a dose," snapped Anita.

Gunther heard a footfall in the hall. He turned around just as Boris Hunter, large, muscular, and mean-eyed, came loping up to the door.

"This jasper has the clap!" Anita jerked her thumb toward Dan Gunther.

"Get your pants on, mister!" Boris folded his massive arms in front of his chest. "And be quick about it! We don't cotton to customers with polluted peckers!"

Gunther stood his ground. "Somebody has made a mistake," he insisted.

"The little lady says you're sick," Boris replied.

"I can't be," protested Gunther.

"Here's the proof!" Anita waggled the dirty towel before her.

Gunther shook his head. "All the women I've been with are nice ones."

Anita and Boris laughed.

Boris grinned. "That's what everyone says." Then the smile vanished from his face. "Two minutes, buster! Get your pants and boots on. Snap to it, buddy, or I'll mash you like a pissant."

Gunther looked at the size of the man called Boris. He went back into the room and started dressing.

Dan Gunther was waiting in the parlor when Slocum came strolling out of a room. Slocum had enjoyed a delightful fifteen minutes with a blond woman who had given more than his money's worth. Slocum was whistling lightly, was in a good humor, and felt relaxed as all get out.

"Your buddy has a bad case of clap," Boris told Slocum. "The house policy is no refunds."

"You got a dose?" Slocum gave his friend a quizzical look.

"Naw, man. I'm almost a virgin," answered Gunther. "I've only been with two women in my life. My wife and Trixie."

Slocum ignored Gunther and looked over at Boris

Hunter. "Is there a doctor in town who can cure it?"

"Doc Phillips. Upstairs over the bank."

"What's he do for it?" demanded Gunther.

"Doc has a patent medicine that kills the stuff," Boris replied. "If Doc's medicine don't work, then your pecker rots off!"

"Lord," said Slocum.

Gunther made a loud, squawking sound. "I wouldn't let a quack doctor touch me with a ten-foot pole."

Boris chuckled. "It ain't a ten-foot pole you got to be worried about, mister."

"When does the doctor open up in the morning?" Slocum asked.

"I help the doc sometimes," said Boris. "Will your friend be there in the morning?"

"Sure," said Slocum.

"Eight o'clock."

"What do you do for the doc?" Gunther asked.

"Things," said Boris. "Just things. See you boys in the morning."

The early morning sun was clear and bright when Slocum roused for the day. Dan Gunther was still snoring, so Slocum shook the teamster to wakefulness. Gunther got out of his bedroll, pulled on his trousers, and walked to the side of the livery stable to relieve himself. He tried to urinate, but a painful burning sensation spread through his groin. The pain stopped for a moment, then the burning sensation started again.

Gritting his teeth, Gunther buttoned up his trousers and walked over to Slocum. "I can't pass water," he said.

"Well, we'll get the doctor to cure you. Don't worry."

"Hell, I'm petrified."

Deadwood was slowly coming to life as they walked to the center of town and located the bank. Slocum and Gunther sat down on the wooden sidewalk across from the bank. They almost missed seeing a middle-aged man start up the stairway. They crossed the street and followed him.

Sure enough, the slightly plump man went to the top of the stairway, walked down the hall, and inserted a key in the door of an office. The inscription on the door read: Dr. H. D. Phillips, M.D.

They followed the physician into the office.

The doctor removed his hat and hung it on a peg. He was a rumpled man with a stain on the front of his wrinkled white shirt. His long, black-tailed coat needed pressing. His general appearance was that of someone who had been on a month-long binge. His eyes were bloodshot, and his nose was veined with redness.

The doctor's hand shook when he tried to pull a watch from his pocket. "You gents got an appointment?" he asked.

Slocum introduced himself. "Boris said you could cure stuff."

"Boris? Been over to the cathouse, huh? Got throwed out because you got a dose?" The doctor peered at Slocum with his bloodshot eyes. "How bad a case have you got?"

"He's the one with the problem," said Slocum, jerking his head toward Dan Gunther.

"That a fact?" Dr. Phillips looked at Gunther as if he was spoiled meat.

"I can't pass water," said Gunther.

"Bad. Real bad." The doctor pursed his lips. "You got any money?"

"A couple of dollars."

Dr. Phillips shook his head. "You better have more'n that, mister. Medicine costs five dollars. The exam costs another five. Ten dollars to keep your pecker from falling off. Ten dollars is a cheap fee for preserving your manhood. It prevents you from dying of uremic poisoning. That phrase, 'uremic poisoning'—here, Dr. Phillips lowered his voice—"is a high-browed way of saying your piss will back up and poison you. It is a sad and dreadful way to die. In fact, if I had the sense of a village idiot, yours truly would depart this town and take my cure-all to a big city. London. Paris. Perhaps some Oriental country. There I could live like a potentate curing the sexual ills of people who have dallied with scarlet pussy."

Dan Gunther listened to Dr. Phillips's words, but his mind was focused on how Trixie—the strumpet!—could be tortured. He thought of building a huge barbecue spit on the prairie and frying her tail over a fire. Or tie stones to her breasts and throw her into a lake. Or spread gall between her legs and make the woman walk to California. Of course, a man could stake Trixie out on the prairie, smear honey over her pussy, and laugh while the ants drove her crazy.

Gunther's hideous thoughts were interrupted by Slocum's reply to the physician. "We'll pay the ten dollars. Let's get started."

"We have to wait for Boris," declared Dr. Phillips. "I have to look at the patient's pecker. I refuse to perform an examination unless Boris is a witness. I have a good name and a splendid reputation. If I examine a pecker without Boris as witness, a couple of con men might claim I enjoy fondling such extremities. That is absolutely untrue, of course, but some people would believe it. I must have an outside witness who will attest to my scientific neutrality."

"Jesus, Doc, you sure know how to make music with words," said Gunther. "I'm just wondering if you're that good with medicine."

The tread of heavy footsteps sounded in the hallway.

"You're a lucky man," said the doctor. "I'd know the sound of those plodding feet anywhere. Boris has overcome the morning aftereffects of demon rum and gotten his tail here on time."

Smiling broadly, Boris, the hulking, bald-headed brothel owner, walked into the room. His eyes were bloodshot. His whiskey-ladened breath would stop the charge of a buffalo bull at forty yards.

"You ready, Doc?" Boris asked.

"Ah, I see you've had another bout with demon rum," declared the doctor. "This is a bad case. Sorrowful. Really pathetic that men will destroy their health lying with scarlet women. My patient is unable to take a good pee. His system is clogged up. He is going to die unless we open the viaducts for a swift, healthy flood."

Boris made a low, clucking sound with his tongue.

"Come into my examination room, gentlemen," said Dr. Phillips. "Pay no attention to Boris, who is an unrepentant whiskey fiend. But he steers a lot of patients to me. Now, remove your gunbelt and drop your drawers, because we have an exam to do."

"Can you cure me?" asked Gunther in a whining voice.

"Hell, how would I know?" asked the doctor. "Your case is in the hands of the angels. I'll do the best I can, young man, because I truly don't want to see you die. Now, before we proceed there is the matter of ten dollars. Cash. No vouchers. No checks. No I.O.U.'s.

Nothing of a dubious nature is accepted by the management."

"That's a lot of money," said Gunther.

"Don't argue about my fee," declared Dr. Phillips, walking across the room and putting on a white smock. "I missed my morning libation. I can always go to a saloon, get drunk, and forget your problems."

Slocum reached into his pocket, pulled out a ten-dollar gold piece, and laid it on the doctor's desk.

Dr. Phillips seized the coin, inhaled deeply, placed the gold piece between his teeth, and bit down. "Solid gold," he said. "This will buy four bottles of my medicine, more than enough to cure you. My golden nectar will come in handy for social disease, warts, gallstones, and other ailments that afflict you in the future. Okay, Slocum, you go to the back of the room. Now, Mr. Gunther, lay your tool on the edge of my desk. Don't worry, sir! I guarantee you will pass water in a couple of minutes."

Slocum stepped to the back of the room. Dan Gunther dropped his pants and drawers. Meekly and shamefaced, he laid his penis on the edge of the battered oak desk.

Dr. Phillips said, "Take the patient's arms, Boris."

Gunther bristled. "What for?"

"It'll keep you from falling down," declared Boris, seizing Gunther's arms from behind.

"Take a deep breath," said the doctor.

Gunther inhaled.

Then his eyes caught sight of the blurred image of a rubber mallet in the doctor's hand. The mallet was arcing above the physician's shoulder, then moving swiftly downward toward Gunther's penis with a powerful velocity.

A sort of painful gurgling noise started deep down in Gunther's throat.

Behind him, Boris tightened his grip on the teamster's body. The hulking brothel owner pressed forward, forcing the patient to remain in place.

Gunther let out a strangled scream.

He tried to twist away.

Boris held on with his powerful arms.

The mallet struck Gunther's penis with tremendous force.

The teamster felt a blurring sensation of pain.

The shock of the blow spurted through his body.

He yelled like a wounded panther.

Dr. Phillips stepped back nimbly. "Perfect! Hold him, Boris, until he stops screaming. Sir, the worst part is over. The quickest way to a cure is sometimes the most painful. When Boris releases you, step behind the screen and use the slop jar back there. You will get all of that dried stuff out of your pecker when you urinate."

"You sonofabitch!" Gunther twisted in the brothel owner's arms.

Dr. Phillips remained at a safe distance until the pain in Gunther's groin became bearable. Then Boris stepped back and the teamster waddled across the room and disappeared behind the screen. He urinated into a bucket. Although the passage of water was painful, Gunther was pleased to see that the dried substance was being forced out of his member. Maybe, just maybe, it was possible to remain among the living.

While Gunther was relieving himself, Dr. Phillips wrapped up four bottles of his medicine in butcher paper. "The secret of my nectar is a touch of arsenic," Dr. Phillips said. "Don't take too much of it. Follow the directions. Otherwise, you will poison yourself."

Boris laughed. "Mr. Gunther, we sure appreciated your business. Don't you worry none. Doc sounds like a bunco artist, but his medicine really works."

"Indeed it does," added the doctor. "Tell your friends and neighbors to bring their poisoned peckers in."

Gunther pulled his trousers up over his swelling member.

"Painful?" asked Boris.

"Damned right," said the teamster.

Boris laughed. "I enjoy holding patients for the doctor. I get a real charge when they realize that rubber mallet is coming down on their pecker. Like, their bodies get all tense and tighten up. You can feel them starting to get all balled up. But I like holding real tight so they don't twist away."

"Yesiree," said Dr. Phillips. "Working with the first-timers is really great."

"First-timers?" asked Slocum from the back of the room.

"Yeah, they don't realize what's coming," said Dr. Phillips. "You know, we have a real bitch of a time when a patient catches the clap for a second time. Boris has to throw a real hammerlock on them. See, they know what is going to happen. They're dang hard to handle when they're familiar with the mallet treatment."

Boris and the doctor laughed.

Gunther picked up his package of medicine. Slowly, painfully, he turned and walked out of the doctor's office. Slocum tipped his hand to the brim of his hat, said good-bye, and followed his friend down the stairs.

12

"Where is Slocum now?" asked Bart Ramey. The bandit leader rubbed the back of his thumb across the scar on his cheek. He was slumped back in a chair behind a poker table in the Deadwood Welcome Inn, a bucket-of-blood saloon for hardcases and their hangers-on. Ramey had a mild hangover from too much booze and conversation the previous night. Now he had to listen to a strange tale from the worn-out woman who called herself Madam Mamie.

"His bunch is camping out back of the Dakota livery stable," Madam Mamie answered.

"He's with that U.S. marshal, you say?"

"Who won't be any problem for you," said the madam. "He's gone gold crazy. Findlay is a strange man. A lawman, but someone who seems to be looking for a quick way to get rich. He figures this is his chance to hit the jackpot."

"He has to find the place first."

"The Indian will lead him there."

"Then there must be gold in there."

"I think so."

"What makes you feel so sure about it?"

A glint flickered in Madam Mamie's eyes. "I've been selling women for almost twenty-five years, Mr. Ramey. A lady gets a feel for money. I can smell gold in this deal."

"Will you guarantee that?" Ramey looked across the table with hooded eyes.

Madam Mamie sniffed. She picked up her white gloves from the poker table. "I looked you up, Mr. Ramey, because folks said you was a sporting man. Maybe they were wrong."

"Don't get huffy," said Ramey. "Sit down. We can talk a bit about this treasure, try to figure something out."

"That's better." Madam Mamie sat back, raised her blouse, and loosened a stay on her girdle. "Remember, whatever you do, I ride with you. I get my share of the gold. It ain't that I don't trust you, Mr. Ramey. I'm sure you're an honest crook. I've learned, however, it's best to be around when the split is made."

"Fair enough. Maybe we can both get rich."

They talked the heart right out of the morning, punctuating their conversation with shots of peppermint schnapps and beer chasers. Bart Ramey was acquainted with the bartender, so at the bandit leader's signal, a shot of vodka was slipped in each of Madam Mamie's beers. Ramey believed that drunks got befuddled, their brain weakened, and lying became complicated. A drunk was easier to trip up than someone who was sober.

Soon the sparkle vanished from Madam Mamie's eyes. She gushed forth a fluid rush of words about her past. She skipped over her failures and poor choices. Every stumblebum she'd slept with became a wealthy man, a good guy, and someone destined for great deeds. By noontime, Madam Mamie was talking like a magpie, but only an occasional word could be understood.

Bart Ramey motioned for one of his men, who was bellied up to the bar. He ordered the outlaw to accompany Madam Mamie to her house. He promised the woman he would look into Slocum's deal. There might be something to the old gal's story, or it might be as elusive as most of the rumors in a boomtown.

One thing was certain: Bart Ramey needed a big, quick score. Wanted posters for him were tacked up on the walls of every big city and two-bit tank town in the West. The shinplasters carried Bart Ramey's picture, his description, weight, size, and scars. The biggest reward was $10,000 from several bankers' associations. They were upset with Bart Ramey's habit of using six-guns and sawed-off shotguns for withdrawals.

Ramey had heard that Butch Cassidy and the Sundance Kid were holed up safely down in South America. They'd pulled off a couple of sizable holdups, kept the loot, and lit out for a foreign climate. Ramey knew his string was running out, that his luck had been pressed to the limit. He wanted to make a big score and disappear.

The law was slow getting to Deadwood. But when the tin-badge men started showing up, Ramey and his gang would have to move on. Trouble was, free land was running out. The West was filling up. The trappers, hunters, buffalo hunters, and squaw men were becoming part of the past. They were being replaced by homesteaders, settlers, town builders, and folks who got upset with bank robbery, thievery, and other forms of larceny.

Ramey ordered several of his men to keep an eye on Slocum and his group. It was not good if a U.S. marshal was hanging around. If J. J. Findlay lost his gold fever, he might decide to cash in the bounty on Bart Ramey's head.

Reports came in at irregular intervals during that afternoon. Slocum was out on Main Street buying supplies and food for a ride back into the mountains. J. J. Findlay had thrown away his crutch and was walking with the aid of a leg brace pounded together by a blacksmith.

Findlay had gone down to the railroad depot, flashed his badge, and picked up a dozen mailbags. The thick canvas bags would be perfect for carrying gold. Later that afternoon, one of Ramey's men reported that Slocum and his friends would be riding out into the mountains the next morning.

By ten o'clock of the following day, Slocum and his friends were riding through a small valley northwest of Deadwood. They had gotten up early that morning, packed quickly, and set out a half hour after sunrise. Slocum, Findlay, and Big Thunder were in a jovial mood.

Dan Gunther had come along, but the teamster had a sour disposition and was silent. Gunther was worried about his venereal disease. He could pass water easily, but his urinary canal could become stopped up again. He had gone back to see Dr. Phillips and obtained a promise from the physician for a checkup in two weeks. Rather than drink away the time in Deadwood, the teamster decided to accompany the treasure hunters.

Occasionally, the group rode past prospectors working their claims. The hills seemed to be filled with men of every age and description intent on digging for gold. Most were friendly, helpful with advice, and grateful to talk with outsiders. They were usually tight-lipped about how much gold they'd found, but willing to talk on any other subject.

Slocum and his friends stopped for the night by invitation from an old-timer named Angus McWane. A former Kentuckian, the prospector had come west for the California gold rush. He had shipped out of Baltimore with passage to Panama City, then walked across Panama to catch a ship on the western side to San Francisco.

McWane's gray beard hung down almost to his waist. He had erected a small log cabin and nailed together a small corral for his horse and two mules. A few yards down the creek, the old man had put together a small whiskey still. McWane had killed a deer earlier that day and hung the carcass from a tree to drain the blood.

McWane carved off slabs of deer meat to roast over an open fire. "Ain't got around to building a regular fireplace," he explained. "Too busy getting my still fixed up. Being from Kentucky, you know we like a dollop of home brew. You boys help yourself to the squeezin's. It ain't as good as I've made back home, but she'll do up here in God's country."

After eating their fill of deer meat and beans, they gathered in front of McWane's cabin and talked. McWane did not ask where they were headed, following the rules of the gold country.

"This your first shot at prospecting?" Slocum asked.

"Lordy, no! I been to all the big booms," McWane declared. "Californy . . . made a fortune panning on the Feather River and spent every ounce in two weeks of wild living in San Francisco. I was a young'un then and filled with get-up-and-go. I even went to the doodad up on the Frazier River in Canada. Not enough gold to catch under your fingernails, 'n' the folks in San Francisco had to take up a collection to get us home. Next, I went over in Nevada and went through those boomtowns."

"Did you make Virginia City?" Findlay asked.

"Hell, the Comstock lode was something in 'er time," declared McWane. "Fortunes made overnight. I knew ole Pancake Comstock, who claimed to make the find. Pancake was crazier than a loon, a whiskey bum who'd lie and cheat to get his booze. His brain was plumb pickled by rotgut whiskey. But I liked the ole cuss. Nothing false about him. Pancake was a wicked ole sot. He didn't put on airs and pretend to be anything except hisself."

"What is it like to have a lot of gold?" Dan Gunther asked.

"Well, some folks go wild around it," McWane explained. The old man smiled, appreciative for the company, glad to be the center of attention. "I've seen friends fight over a little bit of flake. And I've seen fellows go hog wild. Gold does something to people. It's special. It's the only metal that tests a man's character. Being around it makes you find out exactly who you are. You'll find out how far you're willing to go to be rich."

"Some go a long way, I'll bet," said Dan Gunther.

"Over on the Snake River, I saw a man shoot his

brother rather than share a claim," McWane went on.
"Another time, on the Klamath River in Oregon, a man
worked hisself to death digging it out. He just shoveled
until he keeled over from starvation. Crazy men! They
seem to lose their minds over gold."

"Any pickings around here?" Slocum asked.

McWane pursed his lips and stroked his long beard.
"Some find it," he said. "Others don't. I ain't saying
how I'm doing. But you fellows might consider staying
close by. You'll find color in your pans fairly often."

"We got a place picked out," said Findlay.

"That's nice. Special one?" asked the old man.

"We hope so."

"Thought you might be heading for a special place,"
said McWane. "Nobody carries an Injun along lessen he
knows something."

Everyone laughed, including Big Thunder.

"Careful, old man," grinned the Indian. "I'll have the
squaws take care of you."

McWane took another sip of whiskey. "Indians know
all about the gold in these hills," he said. "I tried nuz-
zling up next to them, but the Sioux don't get too
friendly. They're special people. This land is sacred.
That's what they think. Me? I think maybe they're right.
No need for every get-rich-quick pervert in the country
to rush in here."

"You're here," said Findlay.

"But I care for the land," snapped McWane. "I eat
what I shoot. I don't set the hills on fire. I try and live
with the country, like the Indians do. I seen mining destroy lots of places. The vein runs out and everyone
hurries off to another strike. They leave behind a bunch
of slag heaps, garbage dumps, and littered land."

"I get that feeling sometimes," Slocum agreed. "God, or, as the Sioux would say, the Great Spirit, had a mental lapse when he made white people."

Big Thunder chuckled. "Slocum, you could be a Sioux."

"Bet you've lived with the tribes. Right?" Angus McWane cocked his head and gave Slocum a quizzical look.

"A few times."

"Simple people. Nice people."

Slocum nodded. "I agree."

Big Thunder asked, "Then, why is everyone fighting?"

McWane rubbed the back of his hand over his mouth. "Most white folks are too dumb to live a simple life. They got the gimmes. Gimme a big horse, big house, big everything."

"True," Slocum agreed.

"Well, you fellows can sit up and chin all night," said McWane. "I'm too old. Can't drink like I used to. Oh, yeah"—here, McWane looked directly at the man from Georgia—"I meant to ask. You folks know about that bunch that's following you?"

Findlay sputtered and almost choked on his drink. Big Thunder was impassive. Dan Gunther looked surprised but unconcerned.

"I caught sight of them this afternoon," Slocum said.

Findlay frowned. "Why didn't you say something?"

"I wasn't sure they were following us. We still don't know for sure."

"They are," said McWane. "They got one man leading straight out on point, a couple more riding point to the side. A whole passel of men are hanging back a couple of miles."

"How did you spot them?" Findlay asked.

"The deer." McWane jerked his thumb toward the dead carcass. "I got it on top of the mountain. You can see for miles from up there."

Findlay was angry. "We should have known someone would track us."

Big Thunder spoke up. "They don't know where we're going. I'm the only one who knows that."

"We'll lose them tomorrow," added Slocum. "No sweat. Right, Big Thunder?"

The Indian grunted his assent.

"Plenty of ways of doing that out here," agreed McWane. "More twists, hollows, and angles in these hills than back home in Kentucky. Now I'm turning in for the night. You gents stopper the jug when you get done."

Bart Ramey and his gang made dry camp in a deep gulch about two miles from McWane's cabin. They chewed on beef jerky for supper, washed down with rotgut whiskey. Madam Mamie was upset by the lack of accommodations, the miserable nature of the bandits, and the fact that most of the outlaws had not bathed in several weeks.

Except for Bart Ramey and a young gunslinger with a moon face, the bandits were a sorry lot. Most were illiterate. Two ferret-faced brothers appeared to be feebleminded. A couple of old-timers in ragged clothes, wearing shiny pistols and carrying expensive shotguns, stared at Madam Mamie with lustful glances. The two old men whispered to each other, laughed, and snickered at what appeared to be comments about Madam Mamie.

Madam Mamie liked Bart Ramey because the bandit leader was a personable man. Short and wiry, Ramey was self-conscious about the scar on his cheek. "Talked back to the wrong dude one night," Ramey told her during the ride out of Deadwood. "Snickersnee. Faster'n you could see, he tried to cut me into itty-bitty pieces."

The madam also enjoyed the company of Cullie Nelson, the kid with the moon face. Unlike most of the bandits, the moon-faced kid wore clean clothes, used bay rum, and smelled nice. He also appeared to be fairly well educated.

Cullie remained apart from most of the other members of the gang. Some of the outlaws claimed that Cullie was too highfalutin in his ways. But Madam Mamie figured even if you were traveling with trash, you didn't have to wear ashes and sackcloth.

Bart Ramey assigned the moon-faced kid to protect Madam Mamie during the trip. Now, with their bedrolls spread out for the night, Madam Mamie was pleased with her decision to set Ramey's bunch after Slocum.

"We're going to be real rich," she told Cullie.

The kid grinned. "I heard that talk before."

"We'll get the gold."

"Maybe."

"Bound to be a lot of it."

"It'll either be there, or not."

Madame Mamie asked, "Don't you have any dreams?"

"I used to."

"What happened to them?"

Cullie Nelson grinned, then his expression turned serious. "Dreams never work out, ma'am."

"What does that mean?"

"Just that I don't have high expectations. So I never get disappointed."

"You sound bitter for a young man." A maternal tone came into Madam Mamie's voice.

"Not bitter," Cullie replied. "Just realistic."

"Sounds bitter to me."

He laughed, a sharp little barking sound. "It ain't. Honest. I get more kick out of life than most of Ramey's bunch."

"They give me the creeps."

"Well, see, this ain't much of an outlaw gang," Cullie explained. "Oh, they're mean as a rattlesnake. Hard as cold-tack bread laid on a shelf for a month. They'd soon slit your throat as say hello. Brutal is the word for them. But they been treated mean since the day they was born. Fighting, kicking, and hurting is all they know. They never learned anything else. So they go through life kicking, scratching, spreading the harm and hurt around to other folks."

"You sound like you're different from them."

"Well, I was raised on a nice farm in Iowa by a loving mother and father."

"How'd you end up an outlaw?"

Cullie grinned. "Shoot, I don't know, ma'am. Guess I'm too lazy to work for a living. I've just always been interested in stealing things. Seemed a whole lot easier than grubbing for a living."

"It could be a short life," the madam said. "Bank robbery is sort of frowned upon by most folks."

"That seems to be the problem with thieving," the

kid agreed. "A lot of folks don't cotton to it. But I reckon a man can't satisfy everybody no matter how hard you try."

Madam Mamie decided that, despite his good appearance, the moon-faced kid was as crazy as the other outlaws.

13

Dawn was breaking in the eastern sky when Slocum's group ate a cold breakfast, said farewell to the old man, and left McWane's cabin. They rode north for half an hour, then doubled back in a zigzag trail for a half hour. This meandering maneuver succeeded in confusing Bart Ramey's group, who were hung over from too much booze. Slocum fell back and rode the drag position and discovered the outlaw gang was losing their trail. He caught up with the others and informed Big Thunder that the outlaws were bamboozled.

Big Thunder led them through a large marsh filled with reeds and sedge grass. Beyond that, they entered a small stream, where the water hid the evidence of their passage. By early afternoon they came to a narrowing in the mountains that ended in a small ravine. They rode single-file into the passageway, pushing back the briars and brush hanging from the sides of the slopes.

The ravine ran for almost a half mile, then opened onto a wide valley. Beyond the flatlands, a sharp incline rose up to become the end of a lake. Eons ago, the countryside had been disturbed by violent earth upheavals. The land trembled and shook, rising and falling from the shock of tremendous subterranean pressure.

When the enormous tremors were over, a mass of molten rock and dirt converged into an earthen dam. This was the incline that rose at the far end of the valley. Many centuries in the past, springs and creeks flowed into this empty basin to form the lake. Millions of gallons of water were trapped behind the thin wall overlooking the valley.

Riding out into the valley, Slocum and his friends were awed by the sight of a high cliff rising above the west side of the lake. The smooth rock surface looked as if it had been planed smooth by a master craftsman. The only disturbances in the surface were a couple of ledges and a grassy outcropping near the bottom. About thirty feet from the top of the cliff, almost dead center in the rock, was a small cave shaped like an eye.

"There's your cave," said Big Thunder. "Remember, this is a sacred area for my people. The Sioux say this is the land of the dead. Stories go back as long as any living man can remember. They say that long ago, back in the beginning of time, ghosts lived here. They were unusual ghosts, not wispy and made of fog, but men who spoke an unusual language and wore clothes that were made from hard, shiny rock. The elders of my tribe believe these ghosts are kin to the Great Spirit."

Slocum asked, "Do the legends say what happened to these rock men?"

Big Thunder shook his head. "They are supposed to have lived here for a time, and then they went away."

"White men?" Slocum wondered.

"I don't know."

"God, what beauty," said Dan Gunther. "I don't know about men made from rock, but I know this place hasn't been visited by many white men."

"And only a few Indians," added Big Thunder. "The wise men of my people come here. They camp beside the lake and ask the Great Spirit to answer their problems."

"Does it work?" asked Findlay.

Big Thunder smiled. "The answer lies within the wise man, I believe. He just needs the time of silence to bring it up out of his mind."

"Well, old legends are interesting, gents," said Findlay. He pulled the sheepskin map from his pocket. "If I'm not mistaken, we came for gold. And, by golly, whoever drew this map had to have been in this valley. I offer the opinion, which is just one man's belief, that we'll soon be rich men."

"I hate to disturb the area," said Slocum.

"We don't have to mess things up," Big Thunder said. "We'll check out the cave, take whatever we find, and beat a trail back to Deadwood."

"Hogwash! We're here for gold!" Findlay's comment was sharp. "We'll do whatever we have to in order to find the treasure."

Big Thunder's face tightened, and the Indian started to object. Then he relaxed and chuckled. "Findlay, your mind runs on a single trail."

"Believe it," the marshal said. "Think of all the years those old medicine men have been sitting on the shore of that lake and staring up at that cave. It will be ironic if all that time a treasure lay there for the finder."

"Well, let's go find out whether it exists," said Slocum. "We can make the top of the cliff and camp there."

"How're we getting into the cave?" asked Dan Gunther.

"Drop down by rope," Slocum said. "Ease down until we can swing into the cave. It shouldn't be too hard."

"Just be sure there's someone to pull us back up," said Big Thunder. "A man could kill himself diving out of that cave into the lake."

"Hell, you'd never live through a jump like that," said Findlay. "Your bones would smash to bits when your body hit the water."

The moon-faced kid came racing down the slope, spurring his horse into a fast gallop. He ducked an overhanging branch from a large tree and reined up before the gang of outlaws riding along the trail. Cullie Nelson had been riding point since early morning, after the gang had roused itself to follow Slocum's group.

"They give us the slip, boss," said Nelson.

"You swore you'd keep them in your sight," snapped Bart Ramey. His expression was grim. The outlaw leader didn't plan on going back to Deadwood with empty saddlebags flapping on his horse's flanks.

"Well, they must've seen us following them," Cullie Nelson said. "They started getting fancy. There's a marsh up ahead. They rode into that and lost us."

Madam Mamie whined, "They got to be around here somewhere."

"We'll find them. Don't worry." Bart Ramey's face tightened. He tried to think of an appropriate maneuver. He looked over at the moon-faced kid. "You got any ideas, Cullie?"

The kid shrugged. "You go in a marsh, you come out at one point or another. We just keep checking the country until we run across something that leads us to them."

"Lord, to come this far and then lose it all," moaned Madam Mamie. "It ain't fair."

Cullie Nelson chuckled. "Shucks, ma'am, don't you be a-fretting yourself. We got some ornery varmints in this gang. That's a foregone fact. No dispute about it. But we got some of the best trackers that ever come up the Missouri River. I'll bet we find those rascals' trail before the sun is down."

"Glory! I hope you're right," said Madam mamie. "I could sure use some gold to keep me warm."

"Just keep believing in the power of a good tracker to find the trail," chuckled the moon-faced kid, kicking his horse in the flanks and riding back to his point position.

The climb to the top of the cliff was difficult for both men and horses. Now, Slocum and his friends stood atop the massive rock wall and looked out over the vast expanse of countryside. The view was awe-inspiring, an expanding vista of natural beauty, wilderness, and rugged terrain.

Down below, the surface of the lake shimmered in the afternoon sunlight. The water was calm, serene. A few wild ducks swam along the shoreline, and an occasional fish leaped out of the water, then fell back beneath the shimmering surface.

They unpacked the mules, unsaddled the horses, and hobbled the animals. When the gear was laid out, Slocum reached inside one of the mailbags and pulled out a long length of rope. "Might as well take a look before dark," he said.

"I couldn't wait until morning," said Findlay. "We may be standing on the wealth of the ages."

"Who's going down?" asked Dan Gunther.

"Findlay won't," said Big Thunder. "Not with that leg. Slocum and I can go down."

"Gunther and I can run things topside," said the marshal.

The teamster stepped to the edge of the cliff and looked down. "Not as bad as it looks," he said. "There's an outcropping. Almost like a set of steps formed in the side."

"Can we use them?" asked Big Thunder.

"If you clean off the weeds," the teamster replied. "They're not too level. But they'll give you something to rest on going down and a toehold coming up."

"Fair enough," said the Indian.

Slocum tied an end of the rope to a tree, tested the knot, and threw the other end over the cliff. "How's it look?" he asked.

Big Thunder peered over the edge. "We got an extra fifteen feet of line. It ought to work."

"Let's hope the cave is level," Slocum said.

"Check it when we get there," the Indian said. "I'm going down. I want to see what's down there."

"I'll be right behind you," Slocum told him.

Big Thunder took a firm grip on the rope, turned his back, and dropped over the edge.

Slocum waited on top until the Indian yelled that his descent had been successful. Then the man from Georgia did not hesitate. He wiped his palms on the sides of his jeans, tested the rope for safety, and went down.

Big Thunder was waiting at the mouth of the eye-shaped cave. He was standing in the center of the opening and pulled the rope toward the cave as Slocum came down.

"This looks pretty interesting," grunted the Indian, pulling Slocum in.

Slocum saw that the center of the eyelike opening was about ten feet high.

"She's fairly level. At least it looks like it," said Big Thunder. "And I don't see any sign of snakes. That's always my first fear when I go into a cave."

"Be thankful for their absence." Slocum leaned over the side and yelled back to the top. "Start lowering the supplies," he shouted.

Moments later, he grabbed a bag of supplies lowered down by Findlay and Gunther. The bag contained a lantern, pick, shovel, dynamite and fuses, and a shotgun and ammunition. The half-dozen sticks of dynamite had been purchased from Gene Olson, the man who ran the Deadwood-to-Cheyenne stagecoach station.

The shotgun was a precautionary measure. Although the cave appeared to be high and dry, and free from any wild animals, Slocum felt there might be another entrance. The shotgun could prove useful if they stumbled over a grizzly bear or a nest of rattlesnakes.

Slocum struck a lucifer and lit the wick of the coaloil lantern. He held the light above his head. "Let's go back in."

"I'm right behind you," said the Indian.

"Move slow. We have to be careful. There could be holes in the floor. We don't want to fall in a bottomless pit."

Big Thunder chuckled nervously.

Cautiously, they walked back into the cave. The stone floor was covered with dirt and dust. Large clumps of dried leaves had blown against the walls. One side of the irregularly shaped cave was covered with dried moss. A gray fungus partially covered the opposite wall and a portion of the ceiling.

They had gone about twenty yards into the cave

when the passageway sloped upward. Slocum and Big Thunder moved carefully along the slanting cave floor.

"This is scary," said the Indian.

"Who knows?" Slocum shrugged. "We may be the first people to ever walk along here."

Then the cave dipped at a slanting angle. They walked into a vast cavern that seemed like a subterranean cathedral. The walls of the room were at least fifty feet high. The sides of the chamber soared upward to a conical ceiling. Portions of the walls were covered with spiderwebs that gleamed like silver in the lantern light. The two men paused and looked around the eerie chamber.

"Lord! Look at that!" Big Thunder's quavering voice echoed against the walls.

Slocum turned and saw the skeleton propped against the wall on the left side of the room. The ghastly white bones were clad in polished armor. The metal had rusted in places, but it was primarily a glistening silver color. A metal helmet lay beside the bony fingers. The bones took on a spectral whitish-gray color in the lantern light.

Big Thunder walked over, bent down, and touched a bone protruding from the armored vest. The rib dissolved into a white, powdery dust.

"My god!" said the Indian. "He's been here forever!"

"Longer than we've been alive," said Slocum.

"How did he get here?" There was wonderment in the Indian's voice.

"Some kind of early explorer." Slocum held the lantern higher to get a better look at the skeleton.

"There it is," said Big Thunder suddenly.

Slocum followed the Indian's pointing finger toward a stack of black bricks. The two men hurried over to the pile. Big Thunder started to pick up one of the bricks but was unable to lift it with his hand.

"Heavy," he muttered.

"Let me use my knife," said Slocum.

The man from Georgia placed the lantern on top of the stack. He pulled out his pocketknife, opened the blade, and scratched into the side of a brick. The black outer coating scraped away under the blade. A bright, reddish golden hue came into view.

"Gold!" said Big Thunder. "The map was right!"

"The fellow over there"—Slocum jerked his thumb toward the skeleton—"must have been a Spanish explorer. The Spaniards were always after gold. But I didn't know they ranged this far north. I've heard tales about them down around Taos and in Texas."

"When did they come here?"

"Two or three hundred years ago."

"No wonder that bony gentleman turned to powder."

Slocum scraped at the brick and told Big Thunder about the Spanish quest for the Seven Cities of Gold. The Spanish conquistadors explored large areas of the West in their search for these fabled cities. He recounted some of the legend to Big Thunder, who was busy scraping away the black tarnish from another gold brick.

"This must be pure gold," said the Indian.

"All smelted down," Slocum agreed. "If we took the time, we'd find the remains of an old smelter around here."

Big Thunder frowned. "In the cave?"

"No. I doubt it. Just somewhere in the country around here."

Big Thunder rubbed at the tarnished gold brick. "My people told of men made from rock. That must have

been my ancestors' way of describing the metal suit on
the skeleton."

"There may be more of those skeletons around here,"
Slocum added. "Do you want to do any more explor-
ing?"

"Not me," said Big Thunder. "We might get lost."

"There's plenty of gold right here," Slocum pointed
out. He didn't want to go stumbling into the darkness
beyond the great cavern. He was jumpy from being
down in the cave. "We got more gold in this pile than
we can carry out on our pack mules. No need to press
our luck."

"We're all rich." Disbelief edged Big Thunder's sudden realization that the treasure was real.

"We're not bellied up to the assay office yet," Slocum replied. "The map was correct. Findlay was right. I
was skeptical, and I'm still amazed at how this whole
thing worked out."

Big Thunder unrolled a mailbag. "About three bricks
to a bag, I'd judge," he said.

"Findlay's going to go crazy," Slocum laughed.

Big Thunder joined Slocum's laughter, then his expression turned serious. "Can we trust Findlay and
Gunther?" the Indian asked.

"Don't go edgy on me."

"I'm serious," said Big Thunder. "Remember what
old man McWane said about gold testing a man's character."

"You want some life insurance?" Slocum asked.

"It might be wise. We don't know how Findlay and
Gunther are going to react."

"You think they would leave us in the cave?"

"They're working the topside," said the Indian. "It

might get awful tempting to cut the rope after we've passed up this pile of gold."

Slocum looked grim. "You're kidding?"

Big Thunder shook his head. "We don't know how they're going to react to all this gold."

Slocum sat down on the pile of gold bricks. He thought over his experiences since leaving his father's farm in Calhoun County, Georgia. The images of men, women—all sizes, shapes, and colors—flooded into his mind's eye. Some had tried to gain money by guile, others by violence. One way or another, they were all hunting for the economic edge to propel them above the ordinary person.

Some had been gunhands who hired out for monthly wages. Others had killed for the bounty on a dead man's head. Still others were like Madam Mamie and her trio of strumpets. People who were willing to violate the moral code to make a handful of money.

Big Thunder interrupted Slocum's thoughts. "Don't think I'm getting jumpy," said the Indian. "I just want to make sure the other fellow doesn't try and outfox me. I don't want to die in this cave. I don't want somebody stumbling on our skeletons another hundred years from now."

Slocum understood the Indian's viewpoint. Wisdom was making sure a man's backside was covered. "We'll send up some of the gold this afternoon," Slocum said. "Then we'll knock off for the day. It'll be getting dark in a little while. Tonight, you switch the mailbags. Put the ones with the gold in a safe hiding place. Fill the same number of bags with rocks. Tomorrow, if anyone takes off, they'll get nothing but rocks for their troubles."

Big Thunder nodded. "It will still leave us stuck down here in the cave."

"I'll snake another rope over the side of the cliff," Slocum explained. "I can do it while we're talking about the gold. I'll tie it to something secure. If I don't get the rope in place, one of us always stays topside. With the rope, we'll always have a way up if anyone goes gold crazy."

"Sounds good," said Big Thunder. He placed a brick of gold in the mailbag. "Don't forget that rope. I keep thinking about what old man McWane said about gold testing a man's character."

When three bricks were in the mailbag, Slocum carried the sack to the mouth of the cave. He tied the end of the rope around the canvas bag and yelled up for Findlay and Gunther to raise it up.

Slocum and Big Thunder were filling the second bag when they heard shouts erupt from the top of the cliff.

"They've opened the bag," laughed Slocum.

"Happy days are a-coming," responded the Indian. "Wine, women, and a fine fiddle tune are headed in our direction."

"The wine will be okay," Slocum told him. "And I can certainly use the company and comfort of a good woman. But I hope the fiddle playing is better than that tinny music Olson made back at the stagecoach station."

"Hell, Slocum, you can hire yourself a brass band," laughed Big Thunder. "You're a rich man!"

Three more bags of gold were raised to the clifftop during the next half hour. Then, with the sun dropping behind the mountains in the west, Big Thunder and Slocum crawled out of the cave and let themselves be raised to the top.

Findlay and Gunther were wild-eyed, happy, and jabbering like madmen.

"Slocum, you sonofagun!" cried Findlay, coming forward and slapping the man from Georgia on the back.

"We're rich!" yelled Gunther.

"How much gold is down there?" Findlay wanted to know.

"A lot more than we can carry out," Slocum said.

"Exactly how many bricks?" Findlay did a little one-legged dance.

"We didn't count."

"We were too busy filling bags," laughed Big Thunder.

"You hear that?" Findlay yelled at Gunther. "Too busy filling those mail sacks to count. Lordy! I'd love to go down and see that pile of bricks."

Slocum provided them with an account of the skeleton, outlining his belief that the dead man was a Spanish explorer.

"But how did he come to be down there?" wondered Gunther.

Big Thunder replied, "His buddies pulled out and left him."

14

Bart Ramey closed one eye and peered through the telescope. He took a moment to adjust the focus on the lens, then saw the image of the smooth rock cliff come into view. Although the sunlight was dimming, the bandit could see the distant outline of four figures moving around on top of the cliff.

"We found them," Ramey said. He handed the telescope to Cullie Nelson, the moon-faced kid. "I thought we lost them for sure. Kid, you do good work. That's one hell of a cliff."

"I try." Cullie peered through the telescope. "You reckon they've found anything?"

"Is that spyglass showing you what I said it would?" asked Madam Mamie. "A cave should be in the middle. It has a shape something like an eye."

"You're right, old woman," said Cullie. "It ain't exactly in the middle, but she's sure close enough to win a prize."

Madam Mamie licked her lips. "Land's sake! After

all this time and trouble, you reckon we'll finally hit the jackpot?"

"If they do, we do," promised Bart Ramey.

"How're we going to split it?" asked the woman. "I expect there will be a share for me, another share for you and your bunch. Does fifty-fifty sound about right?"

"Yeah," replied Ramey, "if we was splitting a herd of goats. When it comes to gold, or whatever's up there, I figure we'd better wait and see what we get. What do you think, kid?"

"I don't argue about a split until the bank has been robbed," laughed Cullie Nelson. He looked back at the gang of riders crowding up for a look. "Better put this spyglass away, Bart, or the others will be lining up for a look like yokels. We ought to be charging a nickel a peek. Bet we'd make more than most of these yahoos have ever seen at one time."

"A fair split's a good thing for everyone," Madam Mamie maintained huffily. "I got expenses and a lot of time in on this."

"And I'm the cock-of-the-walk," said Bart Ramey, reaching over and taking the telescope from the kid. "Let's get back out of sight for the night. Maybe, kid, you can get up early in the morning, take a ride out and look around. I don't get a great yearning to ride in there wide open, like we're a bull's-eye ready to be popped off. The trick would be to find a back-door trail leading to the top of that cliff. We could mosey in real quiet and surprise that bunch."

"First flicker of light and I'm gone," Cullie said.

J. J. Findlay's dream was of multicolored light, remembered faces from his past, and good times that were being relived again. In his dream, the good times seemed to go on forever. He was once again a child in the fertile fields of Pennsylvania, running in the yard outside the farmhouse, hearing his mother singing as she hung up newly washed clothes on the rope line in the backyard.

Then he seemed to come out of the dream for a moment, out of the remembered goodness and light, and entered a hushed darkness that seemed like a restful sleep. He was held there in a golden closeness as time and space ceased to exist. His mother was near him in that eternal place, and so was his father, and the happily barking collie pup given to him on his seventh birthday.

Then Findlay came out of his dream with a sudden rousing that caused a little cry to escape from his lips. He opened his eyes and looked up to see John Slocum standing above him.

"Morning," said Slocum. "We'd better get an early start today. We got a lot of gold to bring out of the cave."

"Whew! You gave me a start," said Findlay wistfully. "I was dreaming, I guess. All about my childhood and a dog I used to have. I haven't thought about that collie pup in years. The best dog I ever had. He was a feisty fighter, always willing to go an extra lap."

Slocum left Findlay rubbing sleep from his eyes. The Georgian walked over to Gunther's bedroll and nudged the teamster's shoulder with the toe of his boot. Gunther groaned, then rolled over and opened his eyes. By then, Slocum was crunching across the rock to the back of the camp, where Big Thunder had wrapped himself in a deerskin.

"Good morning, Chief!" Slocum said in a singsong

pitch. "Rise and shine, you lousy redskin! We got gold to get out of that cave."

"Just another five minutes," pleaded the Indian. "I'm tired. I didn't get much sleep last night."

"Sorry for you," Slocum said. "I'm in a good mood this morning and time is a-wasting. We got that gang of cutthroats behind us someplace. We got animals who will need watering before the sun is too high. Best to get out the gold and start packing out."

Grumbling, the Indian threw back the deerskin, stood up, and looked around. "You seen any signs of that bunch following us?"

"Nope."

"Then why worry about them?"

"They were on our tail," answered Slocum. "We don't want to risk a shoot-out when our mules are loaded down with gold. As good as the mules are, they can't move fast with a load. Best we get it and get out."

"He's right," said Gunther, digging around in a pack for something to eat. "You fellows want some of this jerky?"

"It beats starving," said the Indian. He took a strip of the dried meat and chewed off a bite. His face took on a sour expression. "Maybe I'd just as soon starve. Where'd you get this junk?"

"Bought it at a store in Deadwood," said the teamster. "Storekeeper said it was deer meat."

Big Thunder shook his head slowly. "Nope. Not unless the deer have started looking like polecats."

"Aw, it ain't bad," said Gunther. "Try some, Slocum. You'll need some meat in your belly for the day ahead."

They sat around sharing the jerky, washing down the meat with an occasional swig from their canteens. Everyone was in an expansive mood, filled with good feelings, wanting to get loaded up and head back to civilization.

"Everything will change from here on in," said Findlay. He was sitting on a small boulder, chewing a mouthful of jerky, looking out over the cliff. A thin mist was rising up from the surface of the lake, and across the way several ducks flapped and made a takeoff from the water.

"How do you mean?" asked Gunther.

"We're all going to be rich men. Think about that for a minute. What's your heart's desire, Dan?"

The teamster was thoughtful. "I'm just along for the ride. I ain't been thinking much about it. Besides, I'm not getting a share."

"The heck you're not," said Findlay forcefully. "You're part of this operation. You get a share, just like everyone else. I figure we split it four ways. Share and share alike. What do the rest of you think?"

"Fair with me," said Slocum.

"Me too," added Big Thunder. "You're generous."

"You two are taking the risk," Findlay explained. "I wouldn't be here except for Slocum getting me out of Paradise Valley. I went crazy in the head for a while back there. One thing just led to another. Now we're starting out fresh. A clean slate. The past is wiped clean and we got the world with a downhill run. What are you doing with your share, Chief?"

Big Thunder was thoughtful. "Buy a few pussies to stroke, smell, rub against, and play with."

"You'll be able to afford it," laughed Findlay. "What about you, Slocum?"

"Stick some away for the day I quit drifting," he answered. "I think about going back to Georgia, settling down, and buying me a farm in Calhoun County. Get myself a good woman who likes loving, live there, make a little moonshine, raise a big bunch of hound dogs, and sleep in a real bed every night with my feet tucked under a nice warm quilt, and my arm around my woman."

"Gunther?"

The teamster looked over at Findlay with a light smile tugging the edge of his lips. "Pray I'm over the pox. Get my tail back to Cheyenne and, if my share is enough, buy a little ranch and run a few head of cattle. The wife, the kids, and I need to be a family. I ain't been home much this past year. Reckon that's what got me involved with Trixie. A man stays away too long, he forgets what he has back home. So I'll be staying home and plowing my own field."

"Sounds good," said Slocum. "I can't think of a better use of the gold than to bring a family together."

Big Thunder looked at the angle of the morning sun. "Well, let's get to work. We got a pile of bags to fill and a lot of heavy lifting to do. I'll go down first."

Slocum stood up, rolled his head, and made a rolling motion with his shoulders. "I'm ready."

"Oh, Slocum," said Findlay.

"Yeah?" Slocum turned and looked at the marshal.

"That second rope ain't necessary, pal. We're not going to cut the rope when the gold's on top."

Slocum grinned, embarrassed.

"But let's leave it there," Findlay went on. "No profit in tempting the gods."

"Fair enough," said Big Thunder. He grabbed the rope and vanished over the edge of the cliff.

After leaving the dawning sunshine, the cave was sterile and lifeless in the thin lantern light. Slocum shivered inwardly as he passed the skeletal remains of the armored dead man. He wondered what series of events had brought the Spaniard to his death in this cave.

"We've hardly made a dent," said Big Thunder, sitting on the pile of gold. He was still sluggish and not ready to start to work.

Slocum turned up the wick on the lantern. The light increased in brightness. "We'll never get it all out of here in one trip," he said.

"Who cares?" said Big Thunder. "I'm tired. Lord, I was up half the night switching bags."

"I didn't hear you moving around."

Big Thunder sighed. "You're not supposed to hear me, Slocum. That's the whole idea of doing something on the sneak."

The man from Georgia chuckled. "Gold makes everyone a little crazy," he said. "Findlay and Gunther seem fair-minded."

"Yeah. I'm thinking the switch was a bad idea."

"Well, we'll never get all of the gold this trip," Slocum said. "We'd better get to work and get moving. What about a second trip in here?"

The Indian shrugged his thick shoulders. The movement of his muscles caused the braids of his hair to bounce up and down. "Anybody's guess," he answered. "My people would not look favorably on any white men caught around here."

"Fair warning," said Slocum.

A faint call could be heard from the top of the cliff. Slocum walked to the entrance of the cave. Holding the rope, he leaned out and looked up at J. J. Findlay, who was lying on his stomach. The marshal's head jutted out over the edge.

"It sounds like we got company coming," Findlay yelled.

"Strangers?"

"Gunther has gone to check it out."

Slocum was worried. "You want us up there?"

"We can handle it."

"That bunch that was following us!" The teamster's head appeared over the edge. "We'd better pull you up and get out of here!"

"How many?" Slocum asked.

"About a dozen."

Big Thunder came up to the mouth of the cave. "I'll go up first," the Indian said. "You keep the shotgun and back me up."

"Get moving." Slocum handed the rope to the Indian, who started hand-over-hand toward the top.

Slocum watched the Indian's leather mocassins vanish over the edge. The man from Georgia took a firm grasp on the rope.

Suddenly, the rope went slack.

The top end of the line dropped past Slocum.

He stood there for a moment, dumbly looking at the rope dropping down the side of the cliff. He pushed down a feeling of dread, spun around, reached out for the second line.

It was gone.

The sound of an argument came from the top of the cliff.

Slocum heard a gunshot.

Someone screamed.

A shotgun blast erupted up on top.

Slocum leaned out and looked up.

A strange face looked down, a bearded face twisted with malice and anger.

Slocum ducked back as a shotgun barrel came into view.

The gun roared, and buckshot slammed down the side of the cliff.

"He's dead," a guttural voice snarled. "Dead as hell with a head full of lead."

A horrible shriek rang from above, followed by more gunshots and thrashing sounds. It seemed as if a hundred men were fighting on top of the cliff.

A voice shouted. "Hold him! Don't let him draw! Help!"

A revolver cracked.

More thrashing, more gunfire, and someone screamed.

Slocum looked out as a falling body plunged down into the lake.

He tried to identify the body, but was unable to do so.

It was crazy!

He didn't know whether Findlay and Gunther had conspired against the Indian, or whether Bart Ramey's gang had ambushed his friends. One thing was certain, strangers were involved. That meant that outsiders had come into the operation.

The sound of animals being yanked by their reins came from above.

"Let's get going!" someone yelled.

"These bags are dang full," someone else cried.

Slocum swung around the edge of the cave entrance. He pulled his knife and cut away the vegetation growing alongside the little steps leading up to the top.

It was an exaggeration to call the indentations in the stone a series of steps. They were overgrown with weeds and grass, little toe-holds that had once been carved into the stone. As he cleared away the first step,

Slocum wondered whether the tiny ledge had been made by man or nature.

From above, the noise of hooves pounded against the rock surface of the cliff. Gradually, the sound moved away as the animals went in the direction of the slope going down into the valley. Leaning out over the cave opening, Slocum concentrated on scraping away weeds on the second step.

He labored until the first four steps were cleaned. Then it became dangerous to lean out of the cave at a greater angle. Now he would have to step out onto the first step, stand on the slender ledge of stone, maintain his balance, and scrape away the upper steps.

It ws going to be a dangerous undertaking.

The slightest miscalculation would be disastrous.

The tiniest error would cause him to lose his footing.

He would plunge down into the lake.

Yet he did not have a choice. Staying in the cave was certain death. The skeleton of the dead man attested to what lay ahead for the fainthearted.

Slocum took a deep breath, exhaled, holstered his knife, and stepped out onto the tiny toehold.

For an instant, he thought his balance was gone.

He pressed hard against the side of the cliff. Violently, his hands clawed for a hold on the side of the stone slab.

His fingernails scraped and dug into the stone.

Then his body steadied.

He hung on the side of the cliff for a long moment, savoring his good fortune.

Slowly, moving his hands as carefully as possible, Slocum eased the knife out of his holster. He reached his hand over his head and began to scrape away the dead vegetation on another step.

It was going to take hours to ease his way up the cliff.

At any moment, he could lose his hold and plunge to his death.

Suddenly, he heard something slam into the stone near his head.

Next, he heard the explosin of a rifle from the direction of the slope.

My god! They were shooting at him

He was a stationary target!

It wouldn't require a marksman to put a bullet through his body.

The shot would be relatively easy for anyone with a halfwit's knowledge of rifles.

15

Bullets slammed into the side of the cliff as John Slocum eased his way back into the cave. He had to move slowly, careful not to lose his balance, taking time and risking getting picked off by a bullet. When he was safely back inside the cave, Slocum moved out of view behind the stone.

His green eyes flashed with anger as he looked in the direction of the gunfire. A group of men were gathered at the bottom end of the lake. Even at that distance, Slocum recognized members of the Bart Ramey gang. They were walking around the edge of the lake, laughing, watching the entrance of the cave.

Beyond the riflemen were three riders leading a string of pack mules. Mailbags were loaded on the animals, bags that Slocum hoped contained nothing more than rocks placed inside during the night by Big Thunder. Whatever carnage had occurred on top, whatever fate had overtaken his friends, Slocum hoped that there would not be a healthy payoff for the bandits.

Now, one of the men aimed and fired his rifle into the mouth of the cave. The lead slug whined inside the stone wall, then slammed back and forth like a buzzing hornet. Quickly, Slocum moved through the cave into the huge cavern room. The lantern was sitting on top of the pile of gold. The wick was still burning, illuminating the huge room and casting dark shadows as Slocum moved about.

Slocum heard the crack of rifles from outside, winced at the power of lead slugs slamming against the walls. The mouth of the cave was humming like a swarm of bees. It was an eerie feeling to know he was bottled up inside a rock tomb, that the men outside could stay there until he starved to death.

Then, Slocum glanced around the room. He dismissed the shotgun as being a useful weapon. The scattergun was unable to carry for the distance needed. His face brightened and his eyes glinted with excitement at the sight of the dynamite. The sticks of the volatile explosive were lying with the rest of the gear.

Working feverishly, Slocum wrapped the dynamite into a tight bundle, set the fuse, and raced to the entrance. He lit the fuse and, exposing himself for an instant, arced the sputtering bundle of explosives in the direction of the riflemen. He knew the deadly package would not reach the snipers, but the force of the explosion might cause a break in the thin earth wall holding the lake.

The dynamite rose high in the morning air, hung at the apex of its arc, and then plunged down toward the surface of the lake. It fell a long distance from the Ramey gang members. Suddenly, the natural silence of the wilderness was shattered by a gigantic blast.

The dynamite detonated about ten feet from the surface of the lake. The explosion was loud, a deafening roar that slammed against the earthen wall. The bandits dove for cover as the boom echoed through the hills.

Cursing inwardly at his bad luck, Slocum started to turn away. Then, out of the corner of his eyes, he saw the earthen dam give way. The earth closest to the cliff suddenly disappeared under a deluge of water. Like a fast-moving wave, the land holding back the lake began to vanish. A subterranean cracking sound came rumbling up from the bottom of the lake.

The great mass of water was suddenly free of the ancient, forced boundary. With a growling sound, the water leaped forward, and the outlaws were suddenly facing a massive tidal wave of surging water.

Faintly, Slocum heard the bandits cry out in terror as the wall of water surged forward. The outlaws were transfixed by the spectacle of their impending doom. Men raced for their horses, but the animals reared up in terror. Enormous waves of water gushed into the valley, sweeping away everything in its path.

Slocum saw four of the outlaws vanish under a large wave. A slight smile tugged the edges of his lips as a fat man tried to bob atop the water. The outlaw struggled in the water like a drowned rat. The initial wall of water raced across the valley and slammed against the far rise of land. It hung there for an instant, then rushed back across the land.

Then the returning wave met a new wall of water. Instantly, the valley became a boiling mass of swirling eddies and twisting waves. The fat man vanished under one of the surging whirlpools. The water roiled, twisted, and bubbled like liquid in a boiling coffeepot.

Slocum saw the three riders driving the mules through knee-deep water onto high land. The outlaws handling the pack mules had escaped. But now the man from Georgia was free to try to scale the sheer rock cliff. He would not have to attempt the ordeal under the withering fire from sniper rifles.

Slocum paused before starting to scale the rock wall.

Suddenly, a voice boomed out from the top.

"Are you down there?" came the familiar voice of J. J. Findlay.

"I'm here," Slocum said, grateful beyond measure to hear the marshal's voice.

"I'm going to drop a rope down," Findlay said. "I'm wounded. You'll have to pull yourself up."

Moments later, Slocum caught sight of a rope dropping over the edge of the cliff. When he tested the line, he found it was secure, and he quickly raised himself hand-over-hand to the top.

"Welcome," said J. J. Findlay. The marshal's shirt was red with fresh blood. He waved away Slocum's alarm. "Nothing serious. I caught a slug in the shoulder. It'll heal."

"What happened?"

"They killed Big Thunder," said Findlay. He pointed toward the lake. "He was shot and thrown over the side."

Slocum would always remember the Sioux for his courage.

"Gunther?" Slocum asked.

"Shot up," Findlay replied. "He'll make it."

"What happened?"

"They came in the back way," the marshal explained. "They jumped us. They came in shooting."

"What about the mules and bags?" asked Slocum.

"They had their own pack animals," Findlay said. "Ours got scattered along with our horses. You'll have to round them up. Maybe we can get back to Deadwood. The gold is gone. Rich at breakfast time, broke and shot up before noon."

Slocum laughed. "Big Thunder would enjoy this," he said.

He told Findlay about the Sioux warrior switching bags during the night. Ending the story, Slocum asked, "You think we've got time to find the mules, the bags, and pack out of here?"

Findlay grinned. "Hell, yes! I'd like to see the look on those jaspers' faces when they open the bags and find the rocks. They come gunning in here, ripe for a killing party. They grabbed a couple of the gold bricks I'd kept out from last night. They must've figured like I did, that the bags were full of gold. Lord!" And here Findlay laughed again. "They'll even have to pound off the locks I put on the bags. I was getting those snugged on when the shooting started."

Madam Mamie, Bart Ramey, and the moon-faced kid road out of the valley and avoided drowning. They moved out hard and steady for almost an hour, then halted beside a small stream and let their animals drink.

"Don't let 'em drink too much," cautioned Cullie Nelson. His moon face was flushed from the morning's events. "You got to hold 'em back. They'll drink until they bloat. That happens and we're going to be stuck out here."

Madam Mamie gave a vicious tug on the reins of her horse. "Keep back!" Her voice was shrill. "Don't slobber down the whole dang creek!"

Bart Ramey chuckled. "Mamie's a right natural horsewoman. Wouldn't you say so, kid?"

"Reckon she has some real talent," Cullie agreed.

"Why don't we split the pickings right here? I'll take my share of the old bricks and hit the road with one of these mules."

"In for a minute, in for life," Ramey said.

"I'm thinking of moseying back to Iowa," said the kid.

"You're too fast with a gun to be a farmer," the bandit leader said.

"Folks can get kilt back here. So let's split it and split up."

Madam Mamie's eyes narrowed. "How're we splitting? Fifty-fifty for you fellows and half for me? Lemme hold that brick, Bart. I never seen so much gold in one hunk."

One gold brick rested in Cullie Nelson's saddlebag. Another of the heavy smelted forms was in Bart Ramey's warbag. These were the two bricks grabbed from Findlay at the campsite.

Ramey dismissed drooling over the loot. "The getaway's the most important part of a robbery," he said. "Anybody can make people stand and deliver. But it takes real brains and persistence to get away. We'll split the take in Deadwood."

Four days of travel were required for Slocum, Findlay, and Gunther to reach Deadwood. The trip had been slow. One day and night had been spent at old man McWane's cabin. Findlay and Gunther rested, ate heartily, and found enough energy to continue their return journey. As a parting gift, they gave one of the gold bricks to the old man.

When they rode into Deadwood, they found the town in an uproar. A new gold strike had been hit in the gulch. Men were rushing around in a state of agitated excitement. Wearily, Slocum and his friends negotiated their way through the tumultuous crowd.

At last, they rode up to the assay office.

"Payday!" said Findlay. His arm was in a sling fashioned from one of McWane's old bedsheets. "A three-way split on whatever she brings."

"Fair enough," Slocum said. "You want greenbacks or a check?"

"Greenbacks," Findlay replied.

"The same," said Dan Gunther. The teamster's face was pale and drawn from the ordeal. "I'm going to mend up a few days and head home. I don't need to carry anything heavy."

Slocum reached up and untied the leather lines holding the mailbag on his pack mule. He braced himself and let the heavy bag fall over his shoulder.

"Slocum!" The warning came from J. J. Findlay.

The man from Georgia spun around.

Bart Ramey and the moon-faced kid walked out of an alley beside the assayer's building.

"Figured you'd show up here, mister," Ramey said.

The moon-faced kid smiled. His hands were near his holstered pistols.

"You made a dang fool out of me," snapped Ramey. "I carried a bunch of rocks all the way into town. Everybody was watching when we opened the bags. I'm the laughingstock of this town."

"That happens when you take another man's stake," Slocum said. "Sorry about that gang of yours drowning back in the hills. It happens when rats get away from their corner."

"Well, hell, no hard feelings." Bart Ramey smiled. He moved forward toward Slocum.

Suddenly the bandit pretended to stumble. His left

hand streaked across his shirt. A small hideout gun flashed into view.

Slocum twisted under the heaviness of the mailbag. He fell back against a mule, his hands streaking toward his revolver. Ramey fired, but the bullet went wild.

Slocum's six-gun boomed loudly. He had drawn and taken a quick, thrusting shot at Ramey's heart. A red stain appeared on the front of the bandit's shirt. Ramey looked down at the wound for a moment, then his heart stopped beating and he slumped over into the dirt.

Slocum's green eyes flashed at the moon-faced kid.

"You want some of it?" asked the man from Georgia.

"No, sir. I'm just passing through town," answered Cullie Nelson. "About ten minutes from now, you'll find me gone."

"Don't take much longer than that," Slocum said, his voice as hard as tempered steel.

Cullie Nelson touched the brim of his hat. He figured two gold bricks would buy a lot of land back in Blackhawk County, Iowa. "I ain't even stopping to say good-bye to Madam Mamie. She's all cut up, anyways, after fighting with Bart over the gold and rocks. Just give me time to get to my horse back there in the alley. I'll be riding out. I'll take Bart's horse for myself, providing you don't mind."

"Just get," Slocum said.

The moon-faced kid spun on his boot heel and disappeared down the alley.

"Stop him!" yelled Findlay. "Slocum, that's the little fink that shot me up back in Paradise Valley."

"He gave you a break. Remember?"

"Aw, hell. I'd like to see him stretched out on a cold slab," snapped Findlay.

A crowd of men had gathered around the dead body

of Bart Ramey. They were drawn by the excitement of the shoot-out. They stared down at the dead bandit and whispered, jerking a thumb or nodding their heads toward Slocum.

Slocum heard a rich feminine voice call his name. He spun around and saw Sally Ryan pushing her way through the crowd.

"Still up to your mischief, I see," said the entertainer. "Or did you come to Deadwood to take that job I offered? We got into town last night on the stagecoach. We'll be appearing here for a couple of weeks."

Slocum smiled as he recalled the offer made in Cheyenne by the young lady. Take care of me and the girls, she'd said. Well, chances were, J. J. Findlay would enjoy being nursed back to health by Sally and her group of touring beauties.

"Glad to see you," Slocum smiled. "We come all this way for the pleasure."

"I know a liar when I hear one," Sally laughed. "But it is good to see you."

"Sally, give me about a half hour," Slocum said. "I have a few things to sell. Then a friend and I will be over to see you."

She smiled. "I'm at the hotel. The girls and I will be waiting."

Sighing softly, John Slocum turned and carried the bag of gold into the assay office. It was time for a little feminine diversion.

JAKE LOGAN

___	0-425-09088-4	THE BLACKMAIL EXPRESS	$2.50
___	0-425-09111-2	SLOCUM AND THE SILVER RANCH FIGHT	$2.50
___	0-425-09299-2	SLOCUM AND THE LONG WAGON TRAIN	$2.50
___	0-425-09567-3	SLOCUM AND THE ARIZONA COWBOYS	$2.75
___	0-425-09647-5	SIXGUN CEMETERY	$2.75
___	0-425-09783-8	SLOCUM AND THE WILD STALLION CHASE	$2.75
___	0-425-10116-9	SLOCUM AND THE LAREDO SHOWDOWN	$2.75
___	0-425-10419-2	SLOCUM AND THE CHEROKEE MANHUNT	$2.75
___	0-425-10347-1	SIXGUNS AT SILVERADO	$2.75
___	0-425-10555-5	SLOCUM AND THE BLOOD RAGE	$2.75
___	0-425-10635-7	SLOCUM AND THE CRACKER CREEK KILLERS	$2.75
___	0-425-10701-9	SLOCUM AND THE RED RIVER RENEGADES	$2.75
___	0-425-10758-2	SLOCUM AND THE GUNFIGHTER'S GREED	$2.75
___	0-425-10850-3	SIXGUN LAW	$2.75
___	0-425-10889-6	SLOCUM AND THE ARIZONA KIDNAPPERS	$2.95
___	0-425-10935-6	SLOCUM AND THE HANGING TREE	$2.95
___	0-425-10984-4	SLOCUM AND THE ABILENE SWINDLE	$2.95
___	0-425-11233-0	BLOOD AT THE CROSSING	$2.95
___	0-425-11056-7	SLOCUM AND THE BUFFALO HUNTERS	$2.95
___	0-425-11194-6	SLOCUM AND THE PREACHER'S DAUGHTER	$2.95
___	0-425-11265-9	SLOCUM AND THE GUNFIGHTER'S RETURN	$2.95
___	0-425-11314-0	THE RAWHIDE BREED	$2.95

Please send the titles I've checked above. Mail orders to:

BERKLEY PUBLISHING GROUP
390 Murray Hill Pkwy., Dept. B
East Rutherford, NJ 07073

NAME _____

ADDRESS _____

CITY _____

STATE _____ ZIP _____

Please allow 6 weeks for delivery.
Prices are subject to change without notice.

POSTAGE & HANDLING:
$1.00 for one book, $.25 for each
additional. Do not exceed $3.50.

BOOK TOTAL	$_____
SHIPPING & HANDLING	$_____
APPLICABLE SALES TAX (CA, NJ, NY, PA)	$_____
TOTAL AMOUNT DUE	$_____

PAYABLE IN US FUNDS.
(No cash orders accepted.)

21